ROCK, RATTLE & ROLL

LOST IN OBLIVION BOOK 1.5

CARI QUINN
TARYN ELLIOTT

RAINBOW
rage
PUBLISHING

Rock, Rattle & Roll

© 2014 Cari Quinn & Taryn Elliott

Rainbow Rage Publishing

Cover by: LateNite Designs

Photograph by: Lindee Robinson Photography

Models: Denise Emilia & Ali Amine

ISBN: 978-1-940346-41-0

First print edition: July 2014

Second print edition: February 2018

ACKNOWLEDGMENTS

Sometimes we make up fictional places that end up having the same names as actual places. These are our fictional interpretations only. Please grant us leeway if our creative vision isn't true to reality.

To Mom and Dad who taught me that love and laughter go hand in hand from the very beginning. Your love story continues to inspire me every day. I hope you're enjoying each other up there in heaven. You two were always happiest when together.

To my brother who outsnarks me at every turn. Yeah, I love you anyway.

To Cari Quinn who stays up with me for hours to create a fictional world where rock stars are attainable and in our very twisted control. I'm so very glad we got that kernel of an idea onto paper and never looked back.

To Diane, Erin, Jennifer and Carolynn for making all of the words make all of the sense.

To Jennifer S. and Rhianna W. for your mad skills in finding music to expand my playlist. You have no idea how much you helped. This girl cannot write without her music.

CHAPTER ONE

THE GETAWAY

DEACON MCCOY STARED AT HIS PHONE. "C'MON. LIGHT UP. A text—something."

"You're just going to have to go kidnap her."

Deacon glanced over at the couch where Jazz Edwards sat cross-legged tapping away on her laptop. The drummer for their band, Oblivion, was decidedly un-Jazz like tonight wearing old jeans and a simple black t-shirt. Her dark hair was minus the colorful doodads he was used to. Though that could be because they were all subsisting on three hours of sleep at night.

The new album was freaking killing them.

Deacon stepped over his body bag sized duffel by the door and sat beside her. The house they were renting was decidedly smaller than the penthouse they'd been living in for the last six months. First of all it was a house. They'd lived in the city for so long, the idea of a backyard—okay, so it was a small backyard, but it had grass—was the main reason they'd signed the lease. Like the rest of the place, it required a bit of sweat and creativity, but hey...look at that—it didn't require their soul.

Evidently they were saving that for the studio. He was tired as hell, and the writing was going...not well. They were fighting over lyrics, fighting over chord progressions, fighting over damn near everything. And if he didn't get away from the entire band for a few days, he was pretty sure there would be bloodshed.

And not his own.

Possibly Simon's. At least as of noon that day. Yesterday had been Gray. When he'd started snapping at Jazz, Deacon had known it was time to get the hell away from everyone. Yelling at Jazz was like drop-kicking a kitten. Not done. Ever. With Christmas just around the corner, it was a good time to take a break. An even better time to drag his wife away for an actual honeymoon.

Wife.

Shit, it still felt strange on his tongue. Strange in a good way. In the best way, actually.

But there had been no time to write a damn thank you card let alone enjoy being married. The band had dived into the studio practically the day after the ceremony. And Harper McCoy was officially starting a new business. In true Harper fashion, she'd hit the ground running. Donovan Lewis, the head of their new label, Ripper Records, had used her for a last minute dinner party, and that had snowballed into a fledgling roster of clients.

The fact that Donovan seemed to know everyone in the state of freaking California certainly helped. Harper had gone from stressing about finding a client to actually having to turn a few down. Something she'd been loath to do.

But tonight was the last job she had until Christmas Eve. Again, she would be working for Donovan for his big end of the year Christmas bash. So their first Christmas would be full of pastries and canapés and one tired chef that wouldn't feel like celebrating.

They needed this time away. They'd been in high gear since they'd met. And getting their schedules to mesh took an act of Congress, for fuck's sake.

They were going on this honeymoon.

No matter what.

He hauled ass off the couch when his phone's face lit up.

COME NOW OR FOREVER HOLD YOUR PEACE.

"Stop grinning at the phone and go. You're making me sick."

Deacon leaned over and pressed a kiss to Jazz's forehead. "What are you going to do around here without me, Pix?"

"If the rest of them are still breathing when you get back, let's count that as a win."

Deacon crouched in front of her. "Maybe you should get away for a while, too."

"What? And leave all this?" She waved around the room. Purple and red Christmas lights framed the huge bay window that looked down on the Hollywood Hills, with its wild mixture of green and desert. Huge L-shaped couches framed the room, making the living room ideal for practice as much as it was for relaxation. Guitar cases littered every corner, as well as a keyboard, cowbell, drumsticks, and a half dozen amps that formed a semi-circle around the Christmas tree stuffed in the corner closest to the window. In the middle of it all were his kettlebell weights for workouts. Jazz was forever banging on them no matter how many times he took them away from her.

They'd downsized in a big way, yet this place felt far more like a home than the penthouse ever did.

Deacon tugged a lock of her hair. "We're just getting our bearings, Pix."

"Yeah, I know." She sighed and flashed a bright smile his way. It wasn't full Jazz wattage, but it was better. "Go." She unfolded her leg and pushed him in the shoulder with her foot. "Have fun. Don't think about us for a whole week. And if you call and check on me, I will ignore every call and text."

Deacon grinned and stood. "I think I might be otherwise engaged."

This time her grin was a little truer. "I just bet."

He headed to the door. With one last look over his shoulder, he slung the huge duffel over his shoulder as well as the small overnight bag Harper had packed.

They needed this time away. He missed spending time with Harper. Between the late night sessions at the studio and her crack of dawn schedule, they'd done little more than reach for each other in the dark.

He tucked the bags into the beater of a truck they both shared, hopped in, and backed out of the circular driveway. He kept it in low gear as he made his descent onto Mulholland, which brought him back toward the city. Deacon liked living on the outskirts of Los Angeles. He could think, and he could run every day. Two of the things he'd thought were near impossible when they'd been in the heart of L.A. He dug under his seat for the GPS, tossing the bean bag base onto the dash. He'd helped bring supplies to the catering job so he had a good idea where he was going, but the hills were a damn maze.

Ten minutes later, he pulled into the side drive of a multi-million dollar house. Only in Hollywood could you have a servant's entrance be as nice as a middle income home. He parked and waved at Annie. She was loading fat plastic bins into the back of the Sweet & Savory truck. He jumped out to help, but she waved him off.

"Please take her or I'm going to kill her." Annie gave him a smile that was all teeth—mean ones.

Deacon pushed his hair out of his face and rubbed the back of his neck. "That good?"

"I don't know what her problem is, but good luck on the honeymoon, dude."

Deacon tipped his head back. *Things will be fine. You just need to get her out of here and away from work.* He rolled his shoulders and straightened. He went inside and found the kitchen.

Organized chaos greeted him. One of Harper's minions was at the sink taking care of dishes, another organizing leftovers, and then there was his wife...she was slamming trays into the portable bin. The only sounds in the kitchen were of the packing variety.

Which was unusual in itself. Usually Harper had music going and people chattering away.

Oh, boy.

He went up behind her and when she jammed the tray for a third time to get it into the slot, he covered her hand and gently lifted it so I would fall into place. Instead of melting back into him like she usually did, she shrugged him off.

"I had it."

"I'm sure you did, but let's save the tray from annihilation."

She whirled in his arms. "Are you here to pick at me, because I do not need this right now, big guy."

Well, at least the 'big guy' had been in the middle of the snarl. That he could work with. He opened his mouth and she pointed at him.

"Do. Not. Handle. Me."

He shut his mouth. He looked over her shoulder at her workers who were studiously pretending not to stare at them. He caught the girl's gaze at the sink and jerked his head toward the back door. She turned off the sink and gestured to the other worker and they both lifted bins to take outside.

"You didn't just send my people outside, did you?" She turned around. "Where are you going?"

The brunette froze.

Harper's jaw clicked audibly. "Fine," she said through gritted teeth. She turned back to him and drilled her finger into his chest. "You do not come in here and undermine—"

Deacon leaned down and covered her mouth. She jammed her fist into his gut, but he held on and was rewarded with her hot mouth devouring his. He smoothed his hand down her braid and cupped the back of her neck until she went up on her toes and allowed him to gentle the kiss.

She was strung tight and frustration radiated off of her like heat. He felt her shoulders ease, her spine melt, and then her sigh fill his mouth. Then he allowed himself to ease back and cup her face.

5

Her eyelids fluttered open and her wild blue eyes sparked with dampened temper. "You think you're so smart."

He shrugged and kissed the tip of her nose. "Normally I enjoy your temper, but we're getting on a plane."

She braceleted his wrists. "I can't—I've got so much..." She looked around the room.

"Annie's got it."

"It's not Annie's responsibility. It's mine."

"Baby, you hired Annie on because she's capable and can practically read your mind. If we don't go now, she's going to put you in the trunk and drive you off the bi-coastal."

Her blonde brows snapped down. "She wouldn't—" At his raised eyebrow, she shut up. "I haven't been that bad."

He kissed her forehead. "A week of recharging sex by the ocean. This is something we both need. Do you realize I haven't been inside you in four days?"

"No, we..." she trailed off. "Wow, has it been that long? No wonder I've been a bitch," she muttered.

Deacon laughed. "We've both been stressed and tired."

She moved into him, looping her arms around his back. "I got a call to do a job."

He stiffened. She really couldn't turn jobs down unless she was already booked, but fuck. He juggled plans in his mind. Not that he'd made that many. He pretty much wanted Harper and a hammock for eight straight days.

She pulled back and looked up at him. Her lips bending into the brilliant smile that never stopped stealing his breath. "I turned it down."

"I—"

Harper reached up and pressed a finger to his lips. "The fact that you were going to rearrange our honeymoon for me to work is pretty much all I could ever ask for. We need this, big guy. After Christmas it's going to be insane with the studio and my schedule booked out through Valentine's."

"I don't want you to ever feel like I'm putting my shit first again."

She hooked her arm around his neck and dragged him down to cover his mouth with hers. The kiss was blazing hot and hard. The kind of kiss that usually left him naked in about three minutes flat.

Most of the time he could tell when she wanted comfort, when she wanted the long and slow burn of romance, and when she was placating him. But this kind of kiss usually came when they were alone. And it felt like it had been forever since he'd gotten a taste of this side of her.

He gripped a handful of her ass and pulled her tighter to him, hooking her knee up on his hip. They stumbled back against the wide island counter. It was enough to bring him back to the moment and the completely inappropriate timing. This was her freaking job. He tried to pull back, but she boosted herself up. Her strong thighs gripped his hips as she fisted his hair.

Surprise and lust tangled inside his chest and kicked hard. His fingers twisted into the apron strings at her back as he held onto her. His other hand supported her butt as she writhed against him. Eyes crossed and blood humming, he tore his mouth from hers. "Harper."

Heavy lids lifted, leaving her blue eyes barely a sliver against the wide pupils. Her mouth was slick and berry red from their kisses. Instead of hopping down she leaned into him, her mouth hovering over his again.

"Lawless," he whispered against her mouth. Chocolate and mint fanned along his lips. Already, her lids were lowering to take his mouth. "I'm going to kick myself from here to Texas for saying this," he mumbled.

Her full lower lip went white from the pressure of her teeth.

"To hell and back," he said again as her tongue swiped over the swollen flesh.

Harper tightened her legs around him. "There's a pantry. Just five minutes." She scraped her nails along the nape of his neck. Her breath came in a near pant. "Okay, seven. Ten tops."

He wasn't sure what had gotten into her, but he wanted every minute of those ten. Hell, he'd take the five. His cock was going show off the imprint of his zipper for the rest of the night. Things between them were always intense, but the light in her eyes was a little...more. He couldn't explain it.

The reminder alert from his phone trilled. A moan traveled from her lips to his as she tried to drag him under once more. He rested his cheek against hers and hauled in a ragged breath. When she undulated against his belly, he had to gentle his grip on her ass. Fuck, he was going to leave bruises. She had him so goddamn wound.

"Baby. We have this amazing house waiting for us. Just one flight away, I promise."

He could feel her heart racing. Her breaths all but a pant as she finally eased the tension of both arms and legs until she slid down to stand on her two feet again. She coasted her hand down his chest and belly, then cupped his erection.

"I had such plans."

The nip of her nails through denim made him hiss. "Jesus."

"I prefer when you moan my name. Tonight I'll make sure it's the only word you can say."

He tipped his head back as her grip finally loosened and her body heat left him, along with her touch. Whatever had gotten into her, he was hoping for a double time repeat once they got to Galveston.

She untied her apron and dumped it into a white box that held place cards and discarded menus. She turned to him, holding out her hand. "I am so very ready to go on our honeymoon."

CHAPTER TWO

INTENSITY

THE HISS OF HYDRAULICS AND GENTLE BOUNCE OF THE PLANE landing brought Harper around. She didn't even remember falling asleep. She'd sat down next to Deacon, still revved from their little interlude at the Bishop holiday party job.

In fact she'd had definite plans to lure him into the bathroom for an official punch on her mile high club card. But she'd blinked out for the entire three hour ride.

"Hey there."

Deacon looked down at her, his eyes soft and sweet as always. "You were out for the count, champ."

"Yeah. I don't even remember falling asleep." She frowned and looked around at the passengers gathering their belongings. "I didn't snore, did I?"

His eyes twinkled. "No, of course not."

She hunched her shoulders. "Oh man, I did."

He laughed. "Just a purr."

"Ass."

He leaned into her, his kiss gentle. "You've been running on four hours of sleep a night for weeks. I'm glad you got some sleep. I have plans for you, wife."

She sighed at the way he said *wife*, the intent in his green eyes, and the light tease of his fingers coasting along her jaw—all things she'd missed so much lately. Her belly flipped as his hair fell forward curtaining out the world. The fresh scent she always associated with him replaced the stale cabin air in the little pocket he'd formed. "You do, huh?"

"All of them include no clothing." He brushed his mouth over hers. "None."

She let herself fall into him. No rushing, no quick kisses as they passed each other in the morning. Her getting up to work, him coming home from the studio. They had all the time in the world for each other. For a solid week, he was hers and she was his.

He broke away when he was bumped by another passenger. The flight attendant was barking out information about Houston, the airport, the weather. She sighed. "I guess we need to get out of here."

"Looks like." With one more kiss, he stood and grabbed their carry-ons from the overhead compartment. He filled the aisle, halting the forward progression of the people behind him to let her go first.

It really was nice to have her own personal fullback—or was it tight end? She peered up at him and he smiled down at her.

"What?"

"Nothing." She looped her carryon bag over her neck and moved down the aisle. When his hand landed on her ass with a smack, she laughed and hastened her stride.

True to his word, Deacon had kept their wardrobe to a minimum. All they had to wear fit in his travel duffel. They were good at traveling light. She had Galveston and the beach to look forward to, clothing was definitely going to be optional.

She didn't even get cranky as they shuffled down the ramp like cattle. And wonder of wonders the rental car gods were with them too. Deacon had them packed and on the road in no time.

Acres of lights swirled with on-ramps and off-ramps as they left the rental garage and followed signs to the highway. She held Deacon's hand while lights whisked past her window. Her eyelids kept drooping, but she had an endless fascination with runways. She didn't want to miss a moment in the symphony that only the tower could command. Once they hit the monotony of the highway, her eyelids won the battle.

She blinked awake feeling groggy and confused when Deacon smoothed her hair out of her face through the open door. God, she never slept this freaking much.

"Hey there, sleeping beauty."

She rolled her eyes. "I can't believe you let me sleep again."

His face was in stark shadow from the night and the dome light of the car. All angles and amused half-smile. "I didn't let you do anything, Lawless. You were out like a damn light."

"Sorry."

"Don't be. You've been working your tail off for weeks, babe. You needed the rest."

"I know, but it's our honeymoon."

"Not like we could do anything in the car."

She arched a brow.

He laughed and scooped her out of the seat. "We'll save that for inside."

She slipped her arm around his neck. "You're no fun."

"I'm all about the fun. Wait till you see inside."

The first thing she noticed was the fresh, cool briny air. It dragged her back to her wedding day when the ocean and sun had greeted her with the most incredibly perfect day. Having Deacon standing there with the sun at his back was nothing compared to the smile he'd had been wearing the moment their eyes met. It felt like it had taken forever to get down the aisle to him.

If the scent of the ocean brought that memory back every single time, she was totally okay with that. She sniffed and pressed her nose into his neck.

"Hey, what's this?"

"Just remembering a certain day."

"It's a good day, I hope?"

"The best." She nuzzled against the beard that was filling in along his jaw. "November first."

He turned his lips into hers. His kiss was as solid and strong and as intoxicating as it had been when he'd actually asked her marry him in front of her family and their friends.

She cupped his face with her free hand and tasted salt and Deacon there. She gave a watery laugh when he finally pulled back and his eyes were as misty as her own. "God, I love you, big guy."

He closed his eyes for a moment, and they shone even brighter in the dim light a moment later. "I never get tired of hearing that."

She smoothed her thumb over his bearded cheek. The idea that this man didn't know love before them continued to astound her. And now he was hers. As overwhelming as he could be sometimes, he was hers and she'd never change that. "Ready?"

He rounded the car, his long stride eating up the stone walkway dusted with sand. Solar lights led the way with their soft glow. He took the stairs slowly as if he knew she needed to take it all in. Wrought iron scroll work made up a small canopy at the door. Frosted white glass lit up with the same ethereal glow from the path made the old iron light seem otherworldly.

But it was the door that took her breath and made her curl into Deacon tighter. "Oh, wow." Stained an intense and almost iridescent purple, it was a work of art. Made out of heavy wood and huge iron hinges, the door dominated the space, adding to the fairy cottage feel.

"Lila helped me find this place."

"Lila is amazing."

"And she knows it."

Harper laughed. "Put me down. You need two hands to pull that bad boy open."

"I texted the caretaker when we were close, and she came to open it up for us." He hefted her higher, juggling a hand free for one of the large iron rings. "I'm carrying you over the damn threshold."

Delighted, she held on as the twelve foot purple door creaked open. A fresh blast of salt air hit her first, followed by the roar of the tide. The back door was open and diaphanous sheers fluttered in the late night breeze.

It was a small place. The kind of cozy perfection created for honeymooners. A kitchenette filled one corner with gleaming butcher block countertops and dark wood cabinets with oiled brass antique fixtures. A simple pendant light let off a warm glow. Part of her ached to go check it out. She could never quite turn off the cooking side of her, but the huge canopy bed that dominated the main living space blinked out all thoughts of food.

More filmy sheers fell from each corner of the dark four poster structure. A half dozen pillows and a sinfully decadent duvet in frosty white teased them both closer.

"Whoa," Deacon said as he let her slowly slide down to the floor.

She wandered past the bed, sliding her fingertips over the sateen luxury grade bedding. She could feel her husband at her back as if they were both drawn out the French doors. A beautiful pergola strung with white twinkle lights framed out the space, but also left a blanket of stars visible. It was cool, but not cold. A huge hammock swung gently in the breeze off the water.

Winter stark waves ate up the sand leaving a trail of seaweed and foam. It was endless, open and private as only the ocean could be.

Deacon's arms came up and around her. One across her shoulders, the other loosely banded across her belly, enveloping her in his warmth. He rested his chin on the crown of her head and she felt the relaxing exhale of his breath.

"We needed this," she said quietly as she smoothed a hand over his forearm.

He brushed his lips against her cheek before burrowing into her hair that had come out of her braid. He drew in deep, his exhale teasing her neck and shoulder. "I didn't think I'd ever get you alone."

The rumble of his voice made her shiver.

His touch was gentle as the endless tide. A hot trail of breath followed by unhurried lips. She rocked back against him, his solid strength made her feel safe and loved, and his growing hardness at her lower back brought out the urgency from earlier to the forefront.

How he always managed to bring both out at the same time shouldn't surprise her anymore, but each kiss dragged her into the storm that was Deacon. Sometimes a shelter in her own stormy mind, and sometimes he was the cause of her turbulent emotions. Love, lust, and comfort tumbled around her chest in a never-ending cycle.

At the nip of his teeth along her jaw, she drew in a shuddering breath. Her nails dug into his forearm holding her tight as his other hand slid under her shirt to trace circles over her belly. Each slow touch seemed to have the opposite effect inside her. Her blood felt like it was racing through her veins. Everything felt too slow, too claustrophobic. She needed more.

Soft kisses and gentle touches were Deacon's stock in trade and she loved him for it. Loved that he cherished her. But the other side of him was what she needed right now. The pounding surf reverberated in her chest like a double time beat. Heady, thrumming, and mind bending.

She laced her fingers over his and pushed his hand higher to cup her breast. The whisper of familiar callouses over her nipple tightened them to aching points. To have him here like this, no interruptions and no ticking clock should have eased her. Instead, a moan crashed out of her too full chest. She flipped up the cups of her bra and shirt. Struggling to get out of the restriction.

Deacon's breath hitched and his touch went from quiet to firm. He cupped and plucked, his mouth busy along her neck where she loved him to suck and tease.

Still not enough.

She still needed more.

The air slipped over her too warm flesh and collided with Deacon's hot hands.

"Yes." She covered his hands again, holding him to her tighter. It felt like there were a million firing points under her skin and all of them were centered on her nipples. Her head slammed back on his chest as she arched.

The echoing groan rumbled through him and into her. She turned in his arms, grasping at his shoulders. The man was nothing if not in tune with her. He hoisted her up so she could wrap her legs around his hips.

Encouraged by the heavy erection tucked between them, she ground her hips against him. It was the best she could do with all these stupid clothes on. She locked her arms around his neck, her nails scraping up the back of his skull. Silky hair feathered through her fingers. Instead of the cool enjoyment she usually got, it felt like fire licking the backs of her hands.

Spurred on by the unquenchable thirst for him, she covered his mouth with hers. His fingers bit into her hips as the kiss went deep and penetrating. Exactly the way she wanted him.

Deep.

Inside her.

Filling her.

Deacon at his most primal. He seemed to understand that. There had been so little time for them lately. So little connection during the little bits of in between. Between jobs, between lyrics, between sessions, between fights with the band.

Between breathing.

Deacon was her air. When life bombarded and suffocated, just the touch of his warm skin brought balance. Sometimes it was the soft she needed and sometimes it was the desperate.

Right now, she was past desperation. She felt like every atom was vibrating apart.

The sheer curtains slid over her bare shoulder as he headed through the doors. Moonlight gilded his hair, his shoulders, leaving the rest of him in silhouette. Her knees dug into his ribs as he lifted her, his mouth finding her breast, his teeth scoring over her nipple before sucking it deep into the heat of his mouth.

They toppled to the bed and he raced down her chest to her

belly, scoring his calloused fingertips over her skin to the stretchy pants she wore. He dragged them down, his open mouth finding the center of her unerringly.

She bowed up off the bed, crying out his name, every swear word she could think of, every oath as his tongue delved between her lips. As he hollowed her out with each drawing suck, followed by long thorough thrusts of his tongue. Pleasure drowned her, his passion fueled her. All of the screaming atoms vibrated and coiled throughout her body.

The fluid softness of the sheets at her back pulled her under as he splayed her open. She tried to crawl up the bed.

Too much.

She was going to fly apart.

Half on the bed, half off, he curled his arms under her thighs and laced his fingers over her belly. With his thumbs, he opened her too-swollen lips. Long fingers owned her body, strummed her, plucked her, soothed her even as he watched her with wild green eyes.

She tried to buck him off.

Too much.

The growl of the dark, dominant part of Deacon lived there at the edge of the bed, staring up at her. Thrilling, dangerous, life-affirming.

Always too much.

And never enough.

Her name was a guttural groan before he fused his mouth over her clit and sucked.

The air seemed to still and the room drifted away. There was only his eyes, his mouth, and the precipice that they both balanced on.

Mine.

Always mine.

Deacon.

Always Deacon.

CHAPTER THREE

GREED

DETONATION.

It was the only word that rolled around in his mind as his wife came under his mouth. She shuddered and her nails dug into his wrists. As if he would ever let her go as she shook and scrabbled for him. Not a chance in hell.

Her taste was beyond temptation.

It was the ocean and love. It was lust and fire. It was everything and he couldn't get enough. He delved deeper for more, licking along the oh so swollen tissues as she surged under him.

Finally, he clicked back in and shucked his pants and shirt to get on top of her. He tried to roll her over on top of him, but she wasn't interested. Grasping, greedy fingers dug into his shoulders as her legs came around his hips.

"Deacon."

Her voice was harsh and rough. The tones so different than her usual sleepy orgasm voice. She sounded almost in pain.

He braced his arms on either side of her face. "Shhh, baby."

She squirmed under him, grinding her swollen pussy over his

shaft. He groaned, trying to rein in the part that wanted inside. Trying to swim to the surface even as he wanted only to drown in her skin and the hot center of her that always felt like home.

Harper's nails nipped over his back to his ass. "Inside."

"Over me," he said raggedly. He didn't trust himself right now. Her taste filled his mouth, her scent was a moment away from ruling his brain.

And the sounds she was making were like nothing he'd heard before.

He grabbed her hand and pushed it over her head, lacing their fingers. When her other became just as recklessly biting, he dragged it up and stared down at her.

High color stained her cheeks and her eyes were too wide.

"Slow down, baby."

She shook her head and rolled her hips till just the tip of his cock slid inside of her. "Yes." Her fingers tightened over his until they were palm to palm. She rose up, her mouth on his neck, her tongue flicking under his chin and then nipping over to his ear. All of the places she knew to get him off.

"Now, inside me now."

Harper, under him. Begging for him.

He canted his hips forward and groaned, pressing his face into the mattress beside her neck. All the places inside of her that were made for him gripped and sucked him deeper.

She closed her legs around his hips, her heels digging into his back as she rose up under him. Her name was a choked litany of gasps as he gave in.

As if he could ever deny her.

He drove inside of her, his brain shutting down as her slick heat welcomed him again and again. Sweat raced down his back, dripped from his temple and pooled between them. He lost himself to that dark, secret part of him that reveled in her giving body. In finding ways to make her scream his name. He gritted his teeth against the shout drawing up from his spine and pushing against his ribs.

The roar that owned him when he let go.

She was the only one he allowed to see this side of him. Afraid of them as much as he lived for these moments. He rose over her, pinning her hands over her head so that her full, gorgeous breasts were stretched up, the tips a dark raspberry with her excitement.

Meeting the wildness living in her eyes, unable to look away, he pistoned his hips against her welcoming open legs. He let her hands go to hook his arms under her knees.

Needing more.

Needing to be deeper.

He opened her wider, until she allowed every last inch inside her sweet, perfect pussy.

She scrabbled up the bed and he chased her with unerring thrusts. Harper reached for the wide headboard and held on, pushing back on each of his thrusts.

She was there, just on the edge, but she didn't seem to have the ability to go over. And God, she needed to. His name a sob in her throat. He slid lower, pulling back to get down to her and make her come with his mouth, but she grabbed a fistful of his hair, dragging his mouth to hers. "Just you." She snapped her jaws tight until he could see the ache as much as feel it. "I need you filling me up. Please, Deacon."

He nodded and rolled her onto her side, splaying one thigh over his hip as he surged up and inside her from behind. He brought his hand down to where they were joined. She was so swollen that she shuddered and thrashed at his touch.

He tried to be gentle, but she covered his hand with her own until the friction was a hair's breadth away from cruel. She'd become impossibly wetter now, so much so he had trouble staying inside her without a concentrated effort. He pressed his forehead into her neck and bit down on her shoulder. Anything to find that spot she so obviously needed. The slow shudder started and he held on. His thrusts deep and punishing. He was too far gone to hold back.

She closed around him, the grip driving him mad. He had to come. He had to finish or they'd die right here in this bed.

Lungs on fire, his abs shaking with each mini-thrust, he finally felt the shudder work through her. His name was a wordless plea on the air as she curled into herself, and he followed her, winding around her, holding her as the lightning scored down his spine and he finally let go.

Wrung out, his body simply shut down and they both relaxed into boneless sleep.

Hours later, she woke him, the need just as insatiable. Full of tangled whispers and urgency, she rode him until her cries drifted out into the sea soaked night and only the surf answered.

When morning finally intruded, he found himself alone in the middle of a storm tossed bed. Pillows were at the foot of the mattress, the duvet dripped off the edge leaving him in only a scrap of a sheet.

He rolled to his back, stretching diagonal across the king sized bed. His morning erection had been long sated at dawn and again a few hours ago by her hungry mouth, leaving him hollowed out and exhausted.

He couldn't remember her ever being that single-minded before. He was usually the one dragging her back into bed to rest and cuddle whenever their crazy schedules allowed. And usually he was the one to initiate sex these days.

Evidently a clear calendar was just what his wife needed.

What they needed.

And if she couldn't walk correctly when they got home, then so be it.

"What's that smirk for?"

He lifted his head, his smirk widening into a full blown smile as she knelt on the bed, holding a mug of coffee out to him. "Nothing." He sat up. "Thanks."

She curled in front of him on her knees, her eyes dancing over the rim of her mug. She'd filched another one of his tour shirts. This time,

Metallica's Master of Puppets slashed across her chest moving freely with her unencumbered breasts.

"What's with the devil eyes?"

She shrugged. "Just happy."

He leaned forward, feeling the smile in her hazelnut kiss. Instead of pulling back, she crawled over to him and straddled his hips. She put her mug down and stole his.

She shifted the sheets, rolling her hips until his cock stirred to life. All it took was a look, a whisper of her scent...hell, just having her in the room had him hard and aching most of the time. But now, he was almost raw from how many times they'd come together.

She had to be sore.

He groaned as she curled her warm fingers around his shaft. "Lawless."

She smiled and slid the tip of his cock along her slit. She was slick and swollen already and took him inside with ease. Normally he had to go slow the first thrust, but she slid down his cock taking him fully inside.

Her summer sky eyes were wild again. The whites just a little too white, the pupils a little too wide. But he was lost to her a moment later. The rolling glide of her hips dragged him inside the shared space that only they could create.

Gaze locked, bodies one, and sunlight turning her hair into burnished gold, she was everything he'd wanted and never dreamed to have. He wrapped his arms around her back and pulled her flush to him until he could have her mouth, too.

The haunting groan from their endless night together spilled out of her mouth and into his lungs. And she rode him harder, her hips going from fluid to frantic.

Where had he lost her?

She'd been with him and now she was arching away, her knees gripping his hips as her fingers bit into his shoulder. "Deacon."

"Shh, baby. I'm here."

He lowered his grip to her hips and controlled the wild bucking. Christ, he didn't want to hurt her. This angle let her control the depth of his thrust, but there was no control in her. Only the tempestuous Harper that had invaded his dreams and their bed last night

Unsure what to do, but willing to trust his instincts, he whipped the shirt up and off her and went for her throat. Cornsilk hair curled around his cheek as he found the spot that drove her mad.

He tumbled her back on the bed and brought his hand between them, using fingers against the hunger-starved clit that felt far too engorged for the moment.

They were combustible together, yes. But this was way beyond their usual. The way she gasped his name as her nails dug in. It fed the darker side of him that wanted out so very badly, but he tamped it down. Not now.

Right now, he needed to stay focused and find his way through the veil of need that seemed to have her trapped. She wasn't with him, she was simply reacting to a stimulus that was gripping her tighter than even his arms could.

He slid out of her and she scrambled up and into his arms, trying to get him back inside of her.

"Lawless, wait."

"If you don't make me come my brains out, I'm going to—"

"Going to what?"

She huffed and stared into his eyes. The wild seeping out of her with heaving breaths. It was still there—on the fringes like a fox ready to take out a defenseless bunny.

He'd never been a bunny before.

And he'd never seen this cunning side of her.

Instead of denying her, he dumped her on her back and went right for the target she wanted him to concentrate on. He latched his lips over the swollen lips of her pussy and found the sensitive knot.

She arched off the bed, and he used every single trick he knew about Harper. He knew her body better than his own. He knew where to stroke, where to nip, how hard to rub, and when she liked the zip of pain with her pleasure.

Her bucking scream-filled pants were louder than the frantic seagulls outside. And he was hard as a goddamn pike, but he pushed his own need to the back of his mind.

And when she shook under his mouth, when the tremors reached out to her thighs, when she finally bowed up with a strangled breathless shout before crashing back to the bed, completely spent, he finally relaxed.

He crashed next to her, his cheek pressed to her inner thigh as he dragged in equally difficult lungfuls of air.

"Oh, my God. Seriously, what is wrong with me?"

He lifted his head. "I'm not complaining in any way, but wow."

She shifted onto her side and scrunched down to him until their noses touched. "Evidently, I can't get enough of my husband."

He laughed. "Your husband is completely fine with that. As long as you give me five minutes to regroup."

She slid the back of her knuckles over his stiff shaft before tracing his aching head. "Regroup, huh?"

"Purely a physical response to all those sex noises you were making."

She pushed his hair out of his face. "I've missed us."

He brushed his nose along hers, breathing her in before he tasted her swollen mouth. It was easy now. The wild had blown out of her like a summer storm. Okay, so it was more like a category three, but it seemed like she was back to his usual Harper.

The sleepy, cuddly one that he rarely saw these days. When she sighed and nuzzled his cheek, he finally let the last of the weirdness slip away.

"So, what do you want to do today?"

Her blue eyes danced. "Anything I want?"

"Anything that includes us going out into the world."

She stuck out her lower lip and he laughed. "At least for an hour."

"Okay." She lengthened the word into a breathy sigh, before rolling him onto his back and straddling his belly. "I say we go shopping."

He groaned.

She drilled her finger into his side until he jumped. "I want to get stuff to cook for tonight. Where else am I going to get such fresh seafood?"

When his stomach growled, he couldn't deny that it was a good idea. "There's a grill outside on the porch."

"Perfect." She vaulted off him, flashing her truly delicious ass as she crossed the room. "I cut up some fruit to go with the croissants that were on the table. I'm going to take a quick shower."

He rolled off the mattress, dragged on his boxers and wandered over to the little table in the kitchen. Part of him wanted to follow her into the shower, but he wasn't sure he was ready for round eight.

Instead, he found the pineapples and strawberries she'd cut up, along with the fluffy pastries and a carafe of coffee. He took the tray and padded out to the patio and stretched out on one of the loungers.

The sun was already at its zenith and a few people were out on the beach. Winter in Galveston was still beach weather for some, himself included. The sea air tasted like freedom. Not that there wasn't plenty of ocean where they were, but Galveston was nice and remote.

He brushed his palm over the heavy beard he'd let grow in. The chances of someone recognizing him here were slim. After next month, his episode on Something Wilde would pretty much put an end to that. He had a fucking cool tattoo to show for it, but the idea of him on display for a television show was downright disconcerting. When he'd done it, he figured that his segment would be a blip on the radar compared to the other clients Casey would have on the air. Casey Wilde's producers had loved it and the social media angle that Jazz and Harper had created so much that it was now the main ingredient of the show.

He was so fucked.

His tat was in the main credits for the show, for fuck's sake.

He wasn't the type to parade around half naked—that was more Simon's style. But the stage was hot, and more often than not he ended up losing his shirt by the end of a run. Hiding his tats weren't really an option even if he conceded to a tank or muscle shirt. His arms were still on display.

A cool tangle of hair slid over his shoulder, dragging him away from the land of fame and the famous. He grinned up at his wife. She smelled like peaches today. He slid his arm around her waist and dumped her into his lap. She giggled and snagged the bowl of pineapple from the tray before settling against his chest.

"It's nice not to have anything to do."

He nuzzled against her wet hair. "Agreed. It feels like we've been chained to a schedule for months now."

"We have been. I know I gave you shit about pushing for the honeymoon right now, but I'm glad you did."

Deacon tucked his chin on her shoulder. "I think I need to mark this down on our calendar."

"Don't say calendar!"

"All right, all right. So how about we get dressed and go see the lay of the land. Then I can bring you back here, and you can cook for me."

"Oh yeah? Can I?"

"Well, I wouldn't want to take that joy away from you."

"What a guy."

Deacon rose off the chair with her in his arms and tossed her on the bed. Her skin was still flushed from her shower and her summer hair a tumble of messy waves. But it was the pure happiness on her face that caught him like a left hook.

Wow. How long had it been since he'd actually seen that side of her in the last few weeks?

She rolled up on her knees, bright eyes moving into naked territory. He waggled his fingers. "Oh no, you cannot seduce me."

One eyebrow slowly rose in question.

He turned away and headed for the shower. "No way."

"Spoilsport!" she shouted after him.

"Hell yes." Deacon looked down at his dick that was so on board with that plan. "You can play later." Then turned on a cool stream of water.

CHAPTER FOUR

THE DANCE

Harper shoved her feet into flip flops as she pulled her hair up into a messy bun. The wind was kicking up off the shore, so it wasn't worth trying to fuss with herself. Not when she'd be covered in sand in ten minutes anyway.

She adjusted the lemon yellow triangles of her bikini top as Deacon came out of the bathroom. His sharp green eyes followed every move of her hands. That heat sizzled under her skin again.

Wild and euphoric, she'd been binging on her husband for the last twelve hours. She should be more in control at this point, and yet...

She swallowed as he buttoned a linen shirt. She had the oddest sensation to go and climb on top of him, pushing that shirt out of the way so she could get to the miles of tan skin.

Cripes. What had gotten into her? She and Deacon had a healthy sex life since the beginning, but she was pretty sure she was going to go into a sex-induced coma if she went at him again this morning. She was sore and swollen at the same time.

Not a good combo.

She watched him replace his towel with a pair of board shorts and couldn't disguise the smile when she saw the tight fit of the front placket. Her husband was just as buzzed on whatever was in the air here in Galveston.

She slid a crochet cover-up over her suit and cutoffs. "Ready to get a closer look at the coast?"

"Definitely."

She held out her hand and tugged him toward the back door. The early afternoon sun warranted a pair of sunglasses and a quick dash across the hot sand to the coastline.

Deacon's surefooted gait left her in the dust as usual, but instead of wandering ahead of her, he turned around and stripped off his shirt, tossing it on the sand.

Distracted by the whole chest to die for thing, she'd been too slow on the uptake. Deacon went into a half crouch and tucked her over his shoulder. He headed into the spray, dumping them both into the seaweed strewn water.

She screeched at the tangle of hairy seaweed, laughing when he dunked them once more. She came up sputtering and hanging off his shoulders. They splashed around in the water for a few minutes before they trudged back in against the mild undertow.

"I forgot about how much I hate seaweed," she said, peeling the salt-caked waxy greens off her thigh.

He shook out his shirt and draped it over his shoulder. "If we head over to the public beach, it's not as bad there."

She tipped her head up at him, seeing the gleam in his gaze. "You want to take a run, don't you?"

"Kinda."

She rolled her eyes. "It's a sickness, you know this, right?"

"The endorphins are so good though."

"I prefer the ones after sex."

He laughed. "Those are my favorite kind."

"How about we walk over to the public beach? We're on vacation. There's no need to race."

He linked his hands with hers. "All right, Mrs. McCoy."

She rose onto her toes and dragged him down to her mouth. He tasted of salt and sunshine. Her earlier desperation melted like the sugary sand under her feet.

This was what it was supposed to be like. She felt his lips smile under hers as he slung his arm around her shoulder and dragged her in close. They walked through the foamy water for a while then up on the packed sand until they came to the public beach.

Kids screamed as loud as the gulls overhead. Harried parents chased toddlers with spray cans of sunblock.

She peered up at Deacon. Just an hour into the sun, and he was already bronzed with color. His shirt floated behind him, now tucked into his back pocket. She had a ridiculously hot husband.

Surprisingly, no one stopped them, but plenty of women followed him with their eyes. His salt-frizzed hair was a bit shaggier than usual and his aviators disguised enough of his face that they could walk unencumbered. His tattoos were also eye-catchers. Soon enough that tat on his back would be beyond famous. Already people were doing double-takes, but he was moving too fast for people to put two and two together.

She stifled a laugh as a group of teen girls gawked as they walked by.

"What's so funny?"

"Nothing."

He leaned down and mock-bit her neck. "Tell me."

"Just amused by how many women have been lusting after you. I think I witnessed it from every age group at least twice."

"Shut up."

She bumped him with her hip. Deacon wasn't terribly comfortable with the objectification portion of his fame, but hell...he was the one that kept his body in such fine form. What did he expect?

"Hungry?"

She shrugged. Food held little appeal lately. All she did was cook. Though the idea of someone else making something for her had merit. And she did need fuel to keep up with Deacon. "I could eat."

He nodded to the little bar off the beach. "How can we *not* go into a bar with a huge mermaid on the sign?"

"Especially named Rhianna's?"

"You wound me, woman. If you're talking about the song that would be Rhiannon."

"Oh." She laughed. "A thousand pardons."

"I might have to take your ring back."

She elbowed him. "Good luck with that."

His dimple flashed as he slid his shirt on, buttoning the bottom two snaps as they climbed the sandy stairs. The bar was full of reclaimed wood painted and sanded in the shabby beach colors of turquoise, yellow, and marine blue. A gorgeous mermaid mural covered the main wall. Clear glass shelves housed alcohol from rot gut tequila and illegible Russian-named vodka to Cabo Wabo and Grey Goose.

Harper climbed onto one of the stools that had been carved into a conch shell. "This place is great."

Deacon leaned on the wide planked bar top, his elegant fingers sliding over the shellacked surface until he came to the chomped end. He laughed and looked up at the bartender. "Shark?"

She nodded. "Mako."

"Fuck."

The bartender leaned forward on her elbows showing an alarming amount of skin from her coral colored halter top. She pushed purple rimmed glasses up her nose. Heavily mascaraed eyes flirted behind the lenses, aiming right at Deacon. "I'm Jenn, but my friends call me DJ. What can I get you?"

Deacon grinned back at her and tapped his left ring finger on the bar top. "My wife and I are looking for some food and a few drinks."

DJ glanced down at Harper. "Man, lucky girl. How'd you bag Mr. Universe?"

Harper pushed her shades up into her hair. "Coconut chocolate popovers."

The bartender laughed and reached back for the ragged menu in the holder behind the bar. "Now that sounds like a story."

Harper grinned. "Girlfriend, there aren't enough hours left in this day to tell it."

DJ laughed and tapped purple tipped nails on the menu. "Well, if you're some sort of cook—"

"Chef," Deacon said.

The flirty blonde waggled her brows. "Yeah, you might be a bit disappointed with the level of cuisine here. Rhi is better with the beer and tequila than she is the menu."

"I heard that." Came a voice from the back.

"Love you," DJ called back to the little alcove next to the mermaid.

"So what's good?"

She lowered her glasses and looked Deacon over. "You look like you can put it away."

He shrugged.

Harper rolled her eyes. "Yeah, he can. I swear he's got extra storage above his belly and a compartment that fills up his chest too."

"Well, I do love a man that can fill up."

Harper covered her face with her hands.

Deacon laughed and slid his hand into the messy knot of hair at the back of her neck, slowly stroking down between her shoulder blades.

"You guys a fan of clams?"

Harper perked up. "Oceanside clams? Uh, yes."

"We make this awesome sourdough bread bowl for our chowder. Add in a couple of orders of steamed clams and a basket of our bar fries and we might even fill up the big guy."

Harper squinted at the bartender. "I'm the only one that can call him Big Guy."

DJ held up her hands. "All right." She leaned forward conspiratorially. "Is he proportional everywhere?"

"Hey now," Deacon said.

31

Harper grinned and nodded over the woman's shoulder. "Is that Cabo?"

She turned. "I have Blanco and Reposado."

"Do a shot with me and I might tell you."

"Lawless."

Feeling a little wild, she laughed as the bartender snapped two tall shot glasses in front of her.

DJ tucked a lock of hair around her ear. "Oh. This is going to end badly."

"Crack open the Reposado."

"Jesus, Harper." At Deacon's surprised tone, she tossed back the first glass.

"Now that is tequila."

Jenn refilled them. "Tell me everything."

Deacon hunkered down in a seat beside Harper. "Looks like you better pour me one too. Just ring up the bottle."

DJ raised her hand up to a bell and gave it a good pull. The clang brought out a cheer and clap from the regulars.

"What was that for?"

"Anytime we have a bit of the devil in the bar, gotta make it known."

Harper let the gold liquid slide down her throat. There was no burn, just the lick of good alcohol and the thrill of doing something that didn't have any repercussions for once. She was on her damn honeymoon. If she wanted to get a little shit faced on the beach, she damn well could. She took another shot, grabbed Deacon by his scruff heavy cheeks, and dragged him down for a tequila soaked kiss.

When his tongue slid along her lips to gather the last drops, she let herself moan. This was exactly what they needed. She hopped off the barstool and wandered over to the retro fitted jukebox. It looked about seventy years old, but the guts were all high end electronics.

She flicked through the songs, smiling when Deacon came up behind her, his wide hands curling around her hips. "Are you going to cause a ruckus tonight, Lawless?"

"I was thinking about it."

She rolled her hips under his touch as Elvis's raw voice filled the bar. An old song from his '68 comeback special buzzed under her breastbone. She ground her ass against the front of Deacon's board shorts. The proof of his deliciously proportional body rose up and pressed into her lower back.

The last time she'd danced with Deacon had been their wedding reception. And that day had been filled with friends and family pulling them apart every five minutes. Even her first dance felt like it had been barely a blink.

She spun around in his arms and grinned up at him as his strong thigh slid between hers. She rolled her hips in time with the thump, strum of the song. Elvis's pitch perfect voice hummed through her chest and arrowed into her pelvis.

As the song rattled and shook to its end, Deacon dipped her back and laughed his way up her neck. His teeth scraped along the column to her chin where he laid a hot kiss on her lips. Public displays weren't exactly Deacon's stock and trade, but there was enough tequila burning between them, along with a long day of sun to make them both a little reckless.

When the song skipped to a chant-heavy Sting song, she glued herself to Deacon's chest. Cocoa butter and salt swam in her head as he moved his hips in time with hers.

More couples came onto the dance floor until the postage stamp parquet floor was a mindless mass of bodies. As the sun went down and people came in to eat and drink, she and Deacon gorged on clams and tequila. They traded off with large glasses of water to keep them on the edge of fun instead of into sloppy and stupid.

They danced and they laughed, and she'd never felt more alive with her clothes on. When he dragged her onto the dance floor for one last time and a slow song left her arms and body heavy with want, she curled into his chest.

They moved slowly and in time.

There was a room full of people, but they didn't matter. Only

Deacon and his skin under her cheek mattered. The reassuring beat of his heart, the stir of his body, the bronze skin delight that was Deacon's chest. All of it was hers.

And she wanted it to only be hers.

She backed off the dance floor, dragging him with her. "Home," she said quietly.

He nodded and tugged her over to the bar. She stood behind him as he paid. Her fingers slipped under his shirt to the taut muscles of his belly and down to the double knot of his board shorts. The rumble of his groan made her bolder.

Beneath the line of the bar where the shadows lay, she curled her fingers around his shaft that had been half hard for the last hour. She smiled into his linen shirt covered back when he cracked his credit card along the bar top.

"Am I distracting you?"

"Yes," he growled.

She brought her other hand under his shaft and cupped his balls. When Deacon's entire body stiffened, she shushed him. "Now, now."

DJ finally finished ringing them up and Deacon hustled her out the door. The dark beach and roar of the tide were disconcerting at first. It was only a ten minute walk back to their cottage, but it felt like an eternity of sifting sand and darkness. Deacon's hand was tight and sure on hers as they trudged along the coast.

She twirled around in front of him and hopped up until she could hang off his shoulders. The music and the laughter of the crowds faded as he kept walking. She wrapped her legs around his hips and bumped her nose along his.

When he laughed into her mouth, she held on tighter. She rolled her hips against his warm belly, crossing her ankles at the back of his waist.

"I love you."

He stopped, his arms tightening around her.

She brushed her mouth over his. The words came easier now. The emotions that he brought out of her were so mixed with love and happiness, she didn't know how to let them out sometimes. They clogged her throat, they were so overwhelming.

He slanted his mouth along hers as his stride lengthened. She didn't stop kissing him as he brought them home, as his gait became uneven at the top of the dunes outside their cottage. Even when he slowly let her slide to the ground, they didn't stop kissing.

Deacon peeled her cover-up over her head and flung it on the lounger. She ripped at the snaps of his shirt and crouched in front of him to drag her tongue along the line of hair above his navel. His long fingers slid into her hair, dragging her back up to him.

He dipped his mouth down to hers as he loosened her bikini top, letting it fall to the shale floor. He flicked open the button to her shorts, making quick work of them as well. The light breeze off the water made shadows play over his skin, accentuating the muscles of his belly and chest with each sway of the twinkle lights.

"God, the way you look at me."

Her gaze locked on his beautiful face and her breath caught at his rough words. He was all stark angles and intensity. Words were trapped in her chest, but she knew exactly how he felt. Like the world was in his eyes. It was terrifying to have one person be the center of her.

He was her world and she was his.

Deacon slid the backs of his knuckles along her collarbone and down to the slope of her breast to her nipple that stood so tight and swollen just because he was there in front of her. She shuddered as his light touch skidded over the flat of her belly to the curve of her pelvis. He slid a knuckle between the already swollen lips of her slit and groaned.

Shadowed eyes glinted in the low light as he turned his hand, dipping two long fingers inside of her welcoming body. She wanted to throw her head back and lose herself to the feeling, but she couldn't stop watching him watch her.

Gentle and insistent, his touch was everything. Slick with her, he delved back inside of her and out again. Each time, the calloused tips of his fingers left behind a light scrape of an echo that no one could ever make but Deacon.

She grasped his wrist as her balance faltered. God, he felt good inside of her. He didn't touch her anywhere else, just the ever slow glide of his fingers until she couldn't do anything except feel. Except experience the buzz that happened when they were in the same sphere.

She wasn't sure if it was the roar of the ocean or the roar in her head as he patiently drew her down the path of her first quaking release. When she could feel her own walls clasping around his fingers, he dragged her close and covered her mouth. The swallow of his groan of pleasure swirled with her own as his tongue mimicked his fingers.

The moon and shadows held her as tight as Deacon's arms as the first wash of misty pleasure swamped her. Distantly, she heard his board shorts fall into a heap as he backed up, dragging her closer to the hammock. He gingerly curled into the wide canvass contraption and drew her in front of him, her back to his front.

Then there was nothing but the floating feel of Deacon wrapped around her. He shifted her and then there was only fullness. Deacon's wide hand across her belly, holding her tight against him as his cock pulsed inside of her already quaking pussy.

His lips found her neck, his other arm cradled her tight so that his forearm banded beneath her breasts. Cherished. The light sway of the hammock and Deacon's rolling hips extended one orgasm into another until they were one knot of love and lust and emotion.

Her name became part of a litany of soft groans of love and earnest praise as she broke again and again. But she never fell.

He would never let her fall.

Finally, the gentle cadence of his release flowed around her and filled her. She drifted off, her husband still wrapped around her and inside of her.

CHAPTER FIVE

STEAM

DEACON WOKE WITH A GROAN. HIS SKIN WAS SLICK WITH MIST and sweat. Harper was still curled in his arms, but they were more like a sloppy, soggy burrito this morning. Residual tequila sloshed in his gut with each sway of the hammock.

Not good.

He squinted at the gray sky peeking between the slats of the pergola. The light rain was picking up and the breeze off the sea was rocking the hammock dangerously.

Definitely not meant to hold a guy his size all night. He looked around, unsure how to unseat them without landing on the shale covered ground.

When another gust tore through the porch, the creak of the rope made the decision for him. He slapped his hand on the ground as gravity and one hundred and fifteen pounds of Harper tried to slide free.

"Shit!"

Harper gasped and instead of curving into him, she stiffened. He managed to roll them, taking the brunt of the fall on his hip and elbow when they hit the ground.

She shrieked out a laugh as she sprawled across his chest.

Sand and water scraped the hell out of his ass as he tried to sit up. "Nice."

"I'm sorry." She tried to stop laughing, he'd give her that. But she inched up his body and put her face in his neck, her shoulders shaking with repressed laughter. "I'm not laughing at you."

Deacon gave up and flattened on his back. If anyone came by, they were just going to have to look away. Man, he had sand in places he just didn't want to think about.

She hovered over him and flipped her soaked hair out of her face. "What is it with us and rain and mud?"

"It's going to follow us around obviously."

"Well, we *are* in Texas."

He lifted his head, looking down at them then back at her face. "The grass hurt less though."

"Aww, poor baby." She slid off of him, wincing. "Wow, that was a lot of tequila last night."

"Ya think?"

She stood up and all thoughts of tequila left him. She was a pink hued bronze from the sun yesterday. Sand and a few tiny shells stuck to her belly and along the side of her breast. Her hair was a tangle from the sea spray and rain, but that smile.

Damn.

She pointed at him. "No. Get that thought out of your head."

He propped himself up on his forearms. "What thought?"

Harper glanced down at his unmistakable hard-on. "You've gotta be kidding me."

"You kinda look like the mermaid from the bar last night."

"You're a very sick man. I look more like a hungover college student."

He rolled to his side and rose to his knees. "Okay, I can work with that. I've never been a frat guy, but we can play frat boy and sorority girl, if you want. I prefer the helpless mermaid though."

She snickered. "Helpless?"

"Thankful?"

Harper's head fell back with a delighted laugh. She pushed her hair out of her face. "Seriously, though."

"Oh, I'm serious." He leaned forward on his knuckles and got one foot under him. "This big, bad fisherman is going to do unspeakable things to you."

"Deacon." Her voice was full of warning. She glanced at the door then back at him, her gaze tripping over his body, especially his cock, making him even harder. Christ, he missed playing with her. It was so rare to get this side of her lately. He wanted more of it. And would definitely make sure he didn't let them fall back into a rut.

"You're not going to beat me to that door, Lawless."

The tip of her tongue came out at the corner of her mouth and he really had no choice. He shot up, snatching her off her feet before she could move a muscle.

She wiggled in his arms. "Deacon," she shouted and dissolved into giggles as he hauled her into the cottage. "Our stuff."

"Later." He tucked her under his arm, heading for the bathroom.

"You can't manhandle me like a caveman. I'm an independent woman."

He simply looked down at her with a raised brow. "Now I'm a caveman?" And when she broke off in another fit, he laughed with her. "I need to shower off my mermaid and turn her back into a real girl."

"God, you're such an ass."

He set her down and opened the wide glass door to the ceiling to floor shower that made up half of the bathroom. He turned on the water and hit the dial on the full body shower heads that sprayed from each wall.

Dragging her inside, he stood them both under the wide rain style hood in the center, sunk his fingers in her hair, and leaned down to her mouth. With water pouring around them, he kissed her, swallowing her laughter with a healthy amount of sand and salt. When her fingers came around his wrists like they always did, he simply sank into her. Steam, Harper, sweat, and a few aches created a hazy bubble of just them.

He lifted her onto the bench, flipping a few of the wall mounted sprayers to hit them. With the height of the bench, she actually could look him in the eye. She slid her hands into his hair and linked them around his neck. The kiss was wet and slow. He let himself steep in her taste. Long, open-mouthed kisses easy with familiarity and a slow build toward the peace he found only with Harper.

Deacon banded his arms around her back, pulling her flush to his chest. She gasped, and he felt the sandy grit between them. He reached back for the soap, but she stole it from him, soaping up her hands with the simple bar before tucking it behind her on the shelf. She soothed her sudsy hands over his chest, washing away the debris from their trip onto the ground. She lightly scratched her nails through his chest hair and over his pecs, then down to his belly.

He groaned with each nip of her nails over the ridge of his abs and lower into the fuller hair below his navel. Reaching around her for the bar of soap, he covered his hands with hers around his shaft. Each stroke of her hand from root to tip nudged him a little further away from the easy gentleness they were enjoying.

She moved one hand up his belly, back to his chest, but instead of continuing to stroke his cock, she pulled him closer to her thighs that were soapy from contact. His head slid along the slippery wetness of her legs, searching for her. Always searching for a way to get inside her perfect body.

But the angle was wrong. Instead, she trapped him between her thighs, lightly grazing the top of his shaft with her pussy. When she found the rhythm she liked there, she went to work with her hands again.

Over his nipples, up to the wide flatness of his pecs and collarbone to his neck. She rubbed her nose along his scruffy neck, the tip of her tongue rasping through the whorls of hair until she got to his ear.

"This body is mine. Every glorious inch is for me to touch." She nuzzled her cheek against his, tucking his hair around his ear. "Only mine."

He groaned as his hips flexed into the suds they made, but the light friction wasn't enough. Despite the running water, he could feel her coating the top of his dick. Her scent filled the steam. The want between them heady as alcohol.

His arms came up around her back, his hands sliding into her wet hair to drag her to his mouth again. Finesse dissolved under the need to swallow her whole. Peace falling away, replaced with lust that chewed through any gentleness living inside him, leaving it and him in tatters.

She dragged her mouth away from his until she could press her forehead to his. Her eyes were laser blue intense and he knew she was right there with him. She reached between them, her grip firm on his cock. "You make me crazy. How is it that I can never have enough?"

He hissed as he pushed through the tight grip, begging for relief. She angled him up so the head of his cock dipped inside of her. The tissues teasingly close, but still she denied him the one thing he wanted.

Steam and soap made for a precarious balance on tile, but he needed inside of her. Needed to open her wide and take her, to sink into her until nothing remained but them.

He swung her off the bench, wrapping her leg around his hip. She hung onto his shoulders as he pulled her under the rain hood again. His mouth opened her as he wanted her legs opened. She met his tongue thrust for thrust, wrapping her other leg around his hip until she could scissor up and lean on his shoulders. He crashed into the opposite wall, the shower bracket digging into his spine, the jet on high.

He twisted them away, her back to the smooth tile away from the water. The soap was gone and she was there, opening for him. He drove inside her ruthlessly. She gripped his hair, relocated to his neck, then finally his shoulders as she hung on. Her nails dug into his flesh as he pounded her into the tile. The slap of their bodies matched the pelting water. He buried his face into the side of her neck, looking down at where they were joined.

His cock sliding in and out of her, nailing her to the wall again and again. He hooked her knee over his forearm to open her wider. He needed more. To see everything, to fit all of him inside her as only Harper could.

She shook around him, her lips quivering.

"Harper?"

"Don't you stop." She brought her trembling thigh up on his hip, clasping around him. Her lids slid down over her eyes as she held onto him and her cries curled around them.

He wrapped her other leg back around him as he pinned her to the wall with his hips, driving himself deep inside of her.

"More," she said with a shaky breath.

He gripped her thighs, forcing her hips to widen until she was splayed open against the wall.

"Yes. Yes," she hissed. The water had gone cool but it didn't seem to matter. They needed that break in the steam. He groaned as her nipples burned into his chilled skin.

Her cheeks were a high pink and her bottom lip was abused from his mouth and her own scraping teeth. He turned to look for the bench, quickly crossing the small area to sit with her astride him.

He lifted his hips up to meet her and finally he was deep enough. His fingers dug into her ass, dragging her up and down the length of his cock. She looked down at him, her hair slicked back, leaving her face unframed and her uptilted eyes wild.

She shifted over him, her hips rolling endlessly as she took him with merciless strokes. He slapped his hand against the wall next to him in the little alcove. He let her take control, drifted into her rhythm and let it become theirs. Sweat coasted down his spine as he met her on each downswing. His cock relentless, his breathing shallow.

"Fuck," he cried out.

And when she screamed his name, there was nowhere else to go but over the edge with her. Panting, he laid his cheek against her chest and heard the roar of her heartbeat as the last edges of his orgasm hazed his vision.

She collapsed against him, her arms around his neck as she slowly smoothed her fingers through his hair. He curled his arm around her hips to keep her from slipping to the floor in a heap.

Well, maybe that was more for him. Dehydration from tequila and a long hot shower with phenomenal sex probably wasn't the best idea, but who the hell cared? "Jesus, you feel amazing," he said against her breast. He sipped some of the moisture that beaded up on her skin.

She pressed a kiss to his temple then pulled his face away from her chest, cradling his cheeks. "We're going to need a shower to recover from our shower."

He brought her hand to his mouth, seeing the proof of just how long they'd been in there. "We're all pruny. We should probably try and get up."

Harper laughed. "I'm not sure my legs actually work at the moment."

He stood with her, grabbing onto the alcove when black spots danced around his head. "I need a gallon of water and something hugely greasy."

"Oh, yeah. Hey, you liked those pub fries over at Rhianna's?"

"Yeah." He carefully set her down and pulled her back over to the middle of the shower. They quickly soaped up and did the whole hair treatment before stumbling out to the bathroom to fight over the sink for a thorough tooth brushing.

They bumped around each other to dry off, their touches softer and less harried now that they had their shower of magical sex out of their system. Not wanting to deal with his hair, he tied on a bandanna, shoved a pair of shades on his face, and stepped into another pair of board shorts.

When he turned around, Harper was fastening a long gold necklace with glass and metal dangles that hung between her magnificent breasts. She shrugged into a bikini top and the purple triangles with cutouts cupped said perfect breasts, making his mouth water.

She had her arms up above her head, tying her hair into one of her crazy intricate braids. If it was at all possible, she looked even more like a mermaid. When she snapped a rubber band around the ends of her braid, he crossed the room and lifted her up, kissing her soundly.

"You are not getting me naked again," she said and squirmed. "I'm starving, dammit."

He tucked his arms under her butt and lifted her breasts to his eye level. "I'm not sure I should let you out of the house with this whole ensemble on."

She stiffened. "Let me?"

"Way too delectable. How the hell am I going to concentrate? Or better yet, when some punk kid drools over you, how am I not going to kill him?"

"So I should take it off for the safety of others?"

"Definitely."

She relaxed into his arms, playing with the ends of his hair. "Good save. But I'm still wearing it."

He nosed along the triangle and watched her nipple peak. "Jesus, you are so goddamn beautiful it hurts to look at you sometimes."

She cupped the back of his head as he flicked his tongue along the little cutout, then moved over to her nipple and sucked her through the material. He lowered her to the floor and palmed her ass before stepping back. She was wearing tiny white shorts that show-cased her tan legs. "Yeah, I'm so going to have to kill someone today."

Harper grabbed her sunglasses off the bed. "Now you know how I feel twenty-four seven."

Deacon tugged his faded white Led Zeppelin shirt over his head. "Whatever."

She walked by and whacked him on the ass. "C'mon, big guy. Feed me before I expire."

CHAPTER SIX

RIDE THE WAVE

HARPER JUMPED ON DEACON'S SHOULDERS HALFWAY TO Rhianna's. She was worn out, dammit. After a ridiculous piggyback ride that left her sandier and sweatier than when they landed on the ground this morning, she was happy to see the beachfront shack.

The morning rain had mostly burned off, but had lasted long enough that the beach wasn't teeming with people today. In fact, when they schlepped into the bar, only three people were inside.

"We are out of tequila!" DJ called from the bar.

Harper laughed and held a hand over her middle. "No more tequila."

Deacon dropped onto a bar stool beside her, his arms and shoulders pushing her over a bit. They shoved at each other until she slid her arm through his and leaned against him.

"You guys are disgusting."

Harper grinned at DJ. "Honeymoon. We're allowed."

"Oh, is that what yesterday's dance floor fuck-a-thon was?"

Harper turned her head into Deacon's biceps. "God, were we that bad?"

DJ nodded with a serious look on her face. "Of course not."

"Shut up."

"Nah, you two are adorable. If he wasn't taken, I would have kidnapped, I mean...taken him home last night." DJ set two glasses in front of them and nodded to Deacon. "You are the most adorable drunk boy I've ever seen."

Deacon groaned.

Harper grinned. "He really is. He doesn't get sloppy often. Takes a lot to get him drunk."

A light flush stained Deacon's cheeks. "All right, enough about last night."

She leaned up and pressed a kiss into his bearded cheek. "You're *my* sloppy drunk."

He nipped her ear. "This sloppy drunk still managed to make you come your brains out last night."

She lifted her shoulder with a laugh. "I didn't hear you complaining either."

DJ poured a pink concoction into their glasses. Pulverized strawberries floated through the mixture. "No sex talk unless I'm invited into the conversation, dammit."

"What is that?"

"This is our strawberry lemonade. Perfection on a hot day."

Harper squinted at her. "What's the proof?"

"Zero. Virgin. Nada." DJ waggled her eyebrows. "In fact, I make delicious pregnancy pops with it. A lot of moms wander in from the beach."

"Oh." She slid the glass forward and sipped. "Holy lemons."

Deacon took his glass and gulped down half the contents. "Man, that's good."

She glanced at him. "Doesn't it taste really lemony?"

He laughed. "If a lemon was dipped in sugar, sure."

Harper scooped a finger into the ice for a strawberry and popped it into her mouth. Frozen strawberries. Smart. It kept the drink cold without having to water it down with too much ice.

"Stop studying it for a menu."

She looked up at Deacon. "Sorry. Occupational hazard."

DJ propped her elbows on the bar. "That's right. You're a cook, right?"

"Chef."

DJ waggled her fingers. "Right, right. La-di-da."

Harper laughed. She took another sip, but man, it tasted like she was sucking on a lemon proper. "Do you have some iced tea to make it an Arnold Palmer?"

"Your sugar buds must be broken," DJ said as she turned to the cooler behind her. She pulled out another pitcher. "It's only sun tea."

"That's fine." Harper pushed her glass over to DJ. She pulled it back and took another sip. "Better."

Deacon tapped the side of his glass. "I'm going with the strawberry lemonade. It's awesome." Deacon nudged her. "Must be that crazy chef palate."

"Must be." Harper frowned. "I am hungover. Maybe that's it."

"Well, let me get you some Rhi Fries."

"Yes." Harper slapped the bar. "That would be excellent. A gut full of grease will put me back to rights." She slid off the stool. "We're going to go find a booth."

DJ waved at her. "Anywhere you want. I am the one and only master waitress, bartender, and hot girl."

Deacon took both their glasses and followed her to one of the booths along the wall. "You all right?"

"Yeah. Just not used to hangovers anymore, I guess."

"Me neither. We'll give it a rest tonight."

"That's until you're looking for wine later."

Deacon gave her a dimpled grin. "It's your fault. Dragging me to those tastings to fill your stash. Bad idea."

She dropped into one side and snuggled in when Deacon sat beside her instead of across the table. He hooked his arm around her shoulder, dangling his fingers a little too close to her chest.

"Behave."

He swiped his pinkie along the side of her breast. "You sure?"

She shivered and crossed her arms to hide the instant response from her nipples. "Evil."

"I can't help it. Those little cutouts keep drawing my eye right there."

She tipped her head up, nuzzling her nose along his furry chin. When his thumb slid over the cutout, she closed her eyes. What was it about the coastal air? She'd never been so revved up so easily in her life. Just a look from Deacon had her aching and crazy.

He made her want to do things in public, for God's sake.

What, like the kitchen of the Bishop house too? Like that, Harper Lee?

Okay, so that wasn't on the coast. She was just happy to be around Deacon that was all.

She dropped her hand to Deacon's lap. When he stiffened under her touch, she flicked her tongue along his neck. "Not so nice, huh?"

He groaned, shifting his foot up on the wooden casing of the booth to block anyone from seeing her fingers curling around his rapidly hardening shaft.

They should be beyond spent, but it seemed the both of them were more than ready for more. She curled her arm around the inside of his on the table as she scooted closer.

"Lawless."

"It feels good, right?"

He groaned as she tightened on him just as he liked. Deacon liked a firm hand with long, slow strokes. His board shorts were loose fitting enough that she had a little give. She turned her face into his neck. "I wish it was my mouth."

"Fuck," he whispered.

She smiled into his neck. "Just a little bit of teeth down the length until I get to the silky soft head. The slit there that tastes so good, just a hint of you on the tip of my tongue."

His breathing grew more gravelly, groans that meant he was with her completely. God, she loved that sound. She nipped at his Adam's apple. "Then I'd draw you inside until you filled my mouth, easing slowly down my throat."

The tips of his fingers teased the underside of her breast as he looked out at the bar. When he hissed out a dark groan, she gripped him tighter. "Squeezing the base of this thick cock as I take the rest. I love the way you taste. Like the ocean and heat. Always so hot."

"Freaking shit. Lawless, you're killing me here."

"We could go outside. Around back. There's no one around today."

"Harper." His groan broke off as she palmed him.

"Let me."

"Here we go, kids."

Deacon's hand went flat on the table as DJ seemed to materialize in front of them. She dropped a huge plate of fries in front of them. She glanced down at him then back up to their faces. "Honeymoon on hold, ya randy pair."

Harper sat up. She missed his heat already. So hot and hard. She cleared her throat. "Just killing time."

DJ looked from her to him. "Do you have a brother?"

Deacon laughed. "Sorry."

Okay, so maybe his laugh sounded a little strangled. But then again, he was sporting a pretty fierce hard-on.

"Of course you don't." DJ sighed and stole ketchup from another table. "Eat first. Then you can go back to your sex shack."

Harper cleared her throat and snagged a fry from under the melted cheese, bacon, and chives. She dunked it into the cup of Ranch. "Eating," she said and popped it into her mouth.

She sighed, then sat back, chewing quickly. The fry was perfectly crisp with the fluffy potato insides she loved, but what was up with the bacon?

And the Ranch for that matter.

Deacon licked his fingers, his mouth full. That was her husband, quick to change gears to his stomach.

"Does it taste okay to you?"

He flicked his tongue over his thumb to get the last of a dab of Ranch. "You're kidding, right? These are awesome."

"I guess you're getting my bacon."

He frowned. "Are you feeling okay?"

"Yeah. I mean a little murky from the tequila, but I've felt a ton worse before."

He leaned in and pressed his lips to her forehead. "Not warm."

She grinned up at him. "Did you just pull a mom temperature gauge?"

"Don't knock it."

She sat back and picked at the fries. The cheese and fries tasted okay. It was just the bacon. She tried the Ranch again, but held it up to Deacon. "Ranch too."

He closed his teeth around her fry. "The Ranch is perfect."

"What the hell did the tequila do to my tastebuds?"

"I don't know. Wonder if you'll hate other things?" His gaze went to his lap.

"Now that would be a true sacrilege."

"No shit," he muttered.

She elbowed him. He smiled around another fry, the jerk. She ate a few more before leaning back into her seat.

"Not hungry?"

She shook her head. "I guess not."

"Do you want to order something else?"

Harper rested her hand on her belly. It didn't feel upset, but she also didn't feel hungry. She slid the plate in front of Deacon. "No. I'm good." She kissed his cheek. "I'm gonna hit the restroom."

His eyebrows lowered. "Sick?"

"No."

"Are you sure you're okay?"

She patted his cheek. "Relax. I'll be right back." She skirted the table and headed to the back of the bar to the restrooms. Once inside, she went to the sink to splash water on her wrists and finally her face. She patted her cheeks with a paper towel, peering into the mirror.

She didn't look any different. A little pale, but that was to be expected with the amount of alcohol she'd consumed the night before. Then why did she feel off? She didn't even feel that hungover now that she'd had two glasses of DJ's lemonade concoction. Dehydration was long behind her.

Was it a vitamin deficiency? Maybe she'd look up her symptoms on Web MD. When another woman came into the bathroom, she gave her a polite smile and headed back into the bar.

Deacon was finished with their fries and he had a bowl of ice cream waiting for her. She smiled and scooted in next to him. "Chocolate ice cream? You must feel bad for me."

"Hey, I like chocolate too."

She brushed her lips over his. "You like strawberry better."

He shrugged and scooped out a spoonful and held it out to her. "You're the chocoholic. This may not be your favorite Scharffen Berger chips, but I'm sure it will hit the spot."

She opened her mouth, letting the icy treat slide across her tongue before she closed her lips around the stem of the spoon. Inferior chocolate to be sure, but ice cream was ice cream.

She frowned when it slid down her throat with a weird aftertaste. It didn't look freezer burned. Seriously? Ice cream tasted crappy too? Where was the justice?

Unwilling to listen to Deacon worry about her, she scooped up another spoonful. Melting whipped cream and a lonely cherry slid down the sundae glass. She popped the Maraschino cherry into her mouth and forced herself not to grimace.

What the hell?

When her spoon hit glass, she pushed the cup away. "Thanks, babe."

Deacon smoothed his hand down her hair. "How about we head back and take a nap? Maybe both of us will feel better."

"Great idea."

"I already paid for the bill, so we can just boogie."

"That's my guy."

Their walk back to the cottage was quiet. Deacon seemed to always know when she needed chatter and when she needed silence. They held hands, sloshing through the small waves that covered their toes.

When their cottage came into view, he scooped her up and over his shoulder, making her laugh as he climbed the sand dunes into the knee-length grass that bordered the fence to their back porch.

He put her back on her feet at the small outdoor shower so they could de-sand. Kisses and a few trailing touches later, he drew her back inside. In no hurry to do anything other than be with each other, they shucked clothing and slid into the king-sized bed.

Both of them seemed intent on sleeping instead of sex. She snuggled into her favorite spot with Deacon curled around her from the back. The breeze was cool enough that her husband's forcefield of heat actually felt good.

When she woke again, sunset's silky red fingers were streaking the sky. She slipped out of bed and grabbed one of Deacon's T-shirts. She sighed as the sun made its descent into the ocean. Could there be anything more beautiful?

A wide palm slid across her belly and Deacon tucked his chin on top of her head. "So, you mentioned that you were going to cook for me?"

"Is that all you can think about?"

"The three food groups that make up a honeymoon are sex, food and sleep. Guess which one I'm looking for?"

She laughed. "I think I remember reading something about a few fishmongers that were close. Want to explore a little? Take a drive down to the wharf?"

"Now that's a plan."

They got dressed and after a few hit and misses with some apps she used to locate fresh markets, they were driving out of the quaint little area they stayed in. Piers and industrial parks gave way to fishing boats and finally a tiny little shop that was open late. The strong scent of fish, seafood and catch of the day specials met them as they opened the rickety door to the shack-sized place.

"Are you sure about this?"

She elbowed Deacon. "Yes. This is the perfect place. Our selection probably isn't going to be the best this late, but I can make us some fish tacos. Yes." She moved down the aisle to the case. Red snapper would be perfect.

Deacon stood behind her, his hands gentle on her shoulders as she made her order. Such a couple thing to do, but this was probably the first time they'd actually been at a market to make food for *them*. She was usually buying in bulk for catering. Not just a few pounds of fish and shrimp to make her husband a meal.

Twenty minutes later they had veggies from a Mom and Pop store and they were on their way back to the cottage. They chatted over food prep, laughed through an impromptu cooking lesson and sang along to the radio.

It was after nine by the time they'd set the table outside and enjoyed their spread of butter and garlic pan-fried shrimp, citrus-infused snapper tacos and a bottle of Moscato. He plowed through the platter of food and she picked at a single taco.

Deacon frowned. "Is your stomach still bothering you?"

She shrugged. "You know me. I'm always picking and tasting when I cook. I'm half filled up before it's even on the table."

He sipped from his wine. "No more tequila for you."

She grinned and held up her glass. "Agreed."

He clinked his glass against hers and hunched over the table. "Are you enjoying yourself?"

"Yeah. It feels weird to relax, but yes." She tangled her fingers with his and leaned forward. The kiss was sweet and soft and held the crisp pear tones of their wine. She stood and drew him up with her. "Dance with me?"

"Here?"

"Yes, here. You, me and the stars."

He slid his phone out of his pocket and flicked through a few songs until the sweet tones of a piano came from his speakers. John Legend's silky voice flowed out into the night as Deacon curled her into his body. His knee between hers, one arm around her waist and the other up and around her shoulders until she was completely encased in his warmth.

One song slid into another, one kiss into soft touches, soft touches into dreamy sighs. They drifted inside, their lovemaking gentle and easy. Full of love and the indulgence of a night without a schedule or deadline. And they both slept dreamlessly in a tangle of limbs and sheets.

Morning came with a grumbling belly. Harper rolled off the permanent heater that she shared a bed with and to her feet. She snagged one of Deacon's shirts and padded into the kitchen.

She found what was left of the fruit and some yeasty bread that was left in a basket by the caretaker. The bread tasted amazing and she buttered three pieces before she felt full enough to stop. She popped a piece of pineapple in her mouth and immediately spit it out.

What the hell?

She tried a strawberry and that tasted fine. She picked up a piece of the pineapple and sniffed—absolutely fresh. She nibbled off a corner of the wedge she'd sliced and nearly gagged. It was completely sour even though it smelled sweet. Possibly a little too sweet.

She made a pit stop in the bathroom and brushed her teeth, glanced at the clock and winced. It was nearly eleven in the morning, but they'd seen the sunrise before they'd gone to sleep. She climbed onto the bed and maneuvered her way under his arm. He rolled into her, cuddling into her back without waking. The man never had trouble sleeping. Harper smoothed her hand lightly over his wide forearms, unable to shut her brain off.

As tired as she was, sleep just wouldn't come. She should Google her symptoms, but she didn't want to move and wake Deacon. Two trips out of bed would be pushing her luck. She was rarely sick with even a head cold. So why was food suddenly her...

She stopped stroking, her hand clamping on his wrist.

No.

There was no way.

She ducked under his arm, her heartbeat filling her ears and trying to blast its way out of her chest. She glanced over her shoulder, but Deacon flopped onto his stomach and put his head under a pillow.

She padded over to her purse and took out her phone, flicking through her screens until she came to her My Days app. She'd always been as regular as the sun, but with stress and living on the road she'd gotten in the habit of keeping track of her period.

Who wanted to be stuck in Albuquerque without a tampon?

It had to be just a few days. She was just being...six weeks late.

She thumbed back through the month.

No.

She had to have forgotten to put it down. She backed up into the fat little club chair at the end of their bed. Her feet collapsed out from under her and she slithered to the floor.

Pregnant?

She cradled her hand over her flat belly, then curled her knees up into her chest. She couldn't. They hadn't even been together long enough to let the ink on their freaking marriage license dry.

She was twenty-three years old, for fuck's sake.

There was no baby in the plan.

She was on the pill, goddammit.

Ninety-nine percent effective unless it's against the super sperm of one Deacon McCoy. What the hell was he shooting, for God's sake? How did he find the way into her freaking cache of eggs?

The eggs that were supposed to stay right there for at least a few... hell, maybe more than a few years.

She brought her hand over her mouth. They hadn't even discussed children. Did he even want them?

Shouldn't that have been a conversation beforehand, Harper Lee?

Fuck off.

She pressed her forehead into her knees, wrapping her arms around her shins.

Did *she* even want them?

She rolled onto her knees and peeked over the footboard of the bed. Deacon was sprawled out, the sheet pooling around his hips, leaving a wide expanse of deeply tanned back. His armor-like tattoo making him look more warrior than killer bass master of a band.

Her eyes traveled to his wide, palmed hand with the long elegant fingers. Strong, sure hands that would protect and cherish a baby as surely as he did her. Instantly, she knew that.

The gentle giant of a man would make the most amazing father.

He rolled onto his side, his arm flung out looking for her. She quickly jumped to her feet and tucked a pillow beside him. He wound his way around the pillow, and a light snore told her he was still down for the count.

You don't know for sure, Harper Lee. Calm yourself.

She grabbed her purse and found her notebook. She scribbled off a note to tell him she went for a walk and left it in front of the clock beside the bed.

No, she didn't know if she was pregnant. And the only way to tell was to get a freaking test. They were in the most remote area of Galveston, but there had to be a drugstore around there somewhere.

It was better to know before she worried Deacon. Before she worried herself for that matter. They'd both been overloaded with stress for the last few months.

She just needed to go and get a test.

Or three.

Just in case.

She looked back at Deacon. She'd go, get the test, and then she'd deal.

56

Jenn. DJ.

She'd know.

Harper quickly tugged on shorts and a t-shirt and flips before rushing out the back and down the beach. The ten minute walk felt eternal, but finally the fin from Rhianna's mermaid tail sign came into sight.

She climbed the sandy steps and found a dark haired woman behind the bar.

Shit.

"Hi."

"Hi there. Whatya have?"

Tequila.

Oh, my sweet God.

Harper collapsed onto the bar stool and put her head between her legs. What if she *was* pregnant? She'd drank enough tequila to do permanent damage to her own head, what had it done to... She put her hand over her middle. God.

Flashes of health class warnings from school filled her brain. Fetal Alcohol Syndrome? How much drinking would cause that? How much had she drank since she'd gotten pregnant? How many times had she shared a bottle of wine with Deacon at the end of the night or with Annie after a shitty party?

"Miss?"

Harper shot off the stool and knocked over chairs and God knew what else to get to the bathroom. She slammed onto her knees and everything she'd managed to eat came up.

A knock came at her door. "Are you okay?"

"Yes," Harper said and felt another heave tighten her belly. Luckily she hadn't really eaten anything. And she certainly wouldn't be having chocolate ice cream anytime soon.

She heard the faucet run and then a hand with paper towels came under the door.

"Thank you." Harper put the wet towel over her face then along the back of her neck before standing up and opening the door.

The woman with dark hair was leaning back against the counter. "Well, you don't look drunk."

Harper went to the sink at the far end of the counter. "No, I haven't had anything to drink."

"Either that's a truly shitty case of food poisoning, or you have yourself a problem, darlin'."

"Look. I don't want to be rude, but..."

"Mind my own business?"

Harper met the woman's shrewd blue eyes in the mirror. "Yeah."

The woman's eyebrow raised. "You come in my bar and toss your cookies, I kinda make it my business. Especially if you're of the pregnant variety. You do what you want on your own time, but I don't serve pregnant ladies here."

Harper leaned heavily on the sink. "Oh, crap." Her vision blurred and the sob came out of nowhere.

"Ah, hell." The woman backed up and ripped off more paper towels. "Okay, honey. Relax."

Harper reached for the paper towels. "I'm sorry," she said around a hiccup. She blew out a ragged breath and sucked another deep one in. "I just figured out I was pregnant. I don't know if I am for sure. I just got the clue and I—"

I just unknowingly tried to drown it in tequila the other night? Was that what she was supposed to say? Horrified, she bent over and put her head between her knees again.

"Okay, okay." The woman took her by the elbow and led her toward the door. "Done puking?"

"I think so."

She pulled her into the dining room and off to the deck outside. "Elise," the woman shouted. "Get me a glass of water for our friend, huh?"

"I don't want to be a bother."

"Honey, you came into my bar and had a little panic attack. It's no big deal."

"I'm Harper."

"Rhianna. I own this place. You can call me Rhi though."

Harper collapsed into one of the chairs and tipped her head back. Tears were still leaking from her eyes, for God's sake. "I'm sorry. I'll be okay in a minute."

"Is there a reason you came tear-assing into my bar?"

Harper leaned forward until her forehead was touching the table. "I was looking for DJ."

"Oh, so you're one of her friends?"

"No, not really. I don't know why I came down here exactly. I'm on my honeymoon. I left my husband sleeping and just had to get here to talk to DJ. I don't know anyone else." She drew in a stuttering breath. "I don't have anyone to call. God, how freaking pathetic is that?" The only person she was close enough to talk to about this was exactly who she couldn't tell. Jazz would lose her damn mind if she told her. And how could she expect her to keep a secret like this? It affected the entire band, not just them.

Then there was Deacon. He would kill her if she told anyone else before him.

No. She had no one to tell. She could call her mother, but they hadn't been very close in the last five years.

What the hell did that say about her?

That she had no real girlfriends in all of this? She laid her cheek on the table, grateful for the cool surface. "DJ was just the first person I thought of."

"Okay."

Harper sat up. "Look, I know it doesn't make any sense. I panicked. I don't know if I'm pregnant for sure, but I don't know where anything is around here. We've been holed up..."

"Doing what got you into trouble in the first place?"

Harper put her head down in her arms with a muffled scream. Yes. They'd been freaking screwing like there was no tomorrow. And before that, it was in desperate late night moments. "How could this have happened? I'm so good about my birth control. We just got married, for God's sake. I just started a freaking business."

Rhianna closed her hand over her arm. "Honey, you gotta take it down a notch. You're going to hyperventilate."

"Of course I am." She popped her head up to stare into the sympathetic blue eyes of the woman across from her. "I can't be pregnant."

"Did you do the math?"

"Yes." She rubbed her eyes. "I'm probably six weeks-ish."

"And you didn't notice?"

Harper sat back in her chair. "New business."

"Right." Rhi drummed her fingers on the table. "And it isn't just stress?"

"I don't know. I've had weird symptoms for the last few days. I just feel off, you know?" She sighed. "I don't want to freak out my husband if I'm just being a basket case."

Or herself. Because she was so freaking out.

"I just figured she could help. I'm so dumb."

Rhi laughed. "No, you're not. DJ's good people. A bit of a pervert, but that's why we love her."

Harper snorted. "Yeah, too true." She was used to perverts. No wonder she latched onto DJ since they got there.

"She isn't on today."

Harper sagged.

"But I've got her cell. So let's give it a little ring, huh?"

"I don't want to take her away from her day off. I'll just call a cab and go into town."

"Tell you what? If she's not around, I'll take you."

"I can't impose. I shouldn't even do this to DJ. I just—"

"You panicked. I totally get it. I did the same thing once upon a time."

Harper clutched her hands together. "What did you do?"

"I didn't have a husband in the picture. And I'd just started this place." Rhi fiddled with her phone.

Harper's stomach dropped. "Oh, wow."

"It's an option, Harper. You're young. You have plenty of time to have kids. Maybe it's just not the right time."

"I—we haven't even talked about having..." God, she couldn't even say it. What business did she even have saying it? She could barely take care of herself these days.

Cripes, they didn't even have a place of their own.

"Okay, I can see you spiraling. Let me call DJ." Rhi flicked her phone on, and a second later she had it up to her ear.

Harper stood, folding her arms over her middle as she paced the length of the outdoor patio. The ocean lured her to the edge of the deck as she listened to Rhianna talk in low tones to DJ. She leaned on the fat, weathered railing, watching the waves eat their way up the beach.

Rhi came up to stand next to her. "She's on her way."

Harper clasped her fingers together, bringing them to her mouth. She nodded because there wasn't much else she could do.

Rhi squeezed her shoulder and left her alone. Harper wasn't sure how long she stood there watching the tide inch its way up the beach. It felt like she was frozen and everything around her was moving so freaking fast.

CHAPTER SEVEN

JUST BREATHE

"ALL RIGHT, KIDDO. WHAT'S THIS I HEAR, YOU GOT YOURSELF knocked up?"

Harper looked over her shoulder. DJ stood there with her blonde chin-length hair pushed back with fat sunglasses. She was makeup free and looked about sixteen without her bartender uniform on. "Hey."

"That stud has super sperm, huh?"

She let out a laugh that was half sob, half hiccup and turned back to the ocean. Crap. She was not going to cry again.

"Hey now." DJ rushed forward and hooked her arm through hers. "I'm glad you came looking for me. We're going to go do the girl thing and get a pregnancy test and pee on that motherfucker. I have awesome karma. If we don't want a blue plus sign, I can hit you up with some crazy mojo."

Harper sniffed. "I'm sorry to drag you in here on your day off. I just ran out of the cottage and came here. I didn't know what else to do," she whispered.

"Well, you're in luck. I have a shitbox of a car waiting outside and we have a drugstore less than five minutes away. Even better, my apartment is right around the corner from this fantabulous drugstore. You can pee on the stick and we'll figure shit out."

Harper nodded. "Okay."

DJ flung her arm around her shoulder and squeezed. "Every woman has had a pregnancy scare."

Not this woman. Of course Deacon had been the only man she'd ever had unprotected sex with.

DJ steered her off the deck and inside. Harper grabbed her purse, letting DJ lead her out the front to her car. Just like any coastal town, rental houses and hotels crowded the streets right near the water. DJ took a few side roads then they came to a major intersection.

Signs for restaurants and fast food speared up from the street. Congested lanes reminded her that she had no idea how long she'd left Deacon. She dug into her purse, and no message was waiting for her. Was he still sleeping? She didn't even remember what she'd put on the scribbled note for him as to why she was gone.

"Cut it out."

Harper looked to DJ. "Can hear my mental freakout, huh?"

"It's as loud as an air horn." She swung into a small parking lot. "Test first, then we figure out a game plan."

As they parked, Harper's nails dug into her thighs.

"C'mon, Harper."

She nodded, but couldn't make herself move her legs.

DJ came around and opened her door, reaching in to drag her out. "I didn't take you for a coward." DJ's eyebrows rose behind her large shades. "There we go. There's that attitude. In we go."

Harper hooked her purse over her shoulder and wrapped her arms tight at her chest. They walked inside. Lights were insanely bright and all the aisles were perfectly marked. No need to ask for directions to the contraception and pregnancy test aisle. Did they do that on purpose? Hey...let's give them a reminder if they don't use condoms that an entirely different little box was in their future?

Why the hell didn't she listen?

DJ walked ahead of her and stood in front of all the different ones. "Okay." She tapped on three different brands. "These are the ones I've used."

Harper's eyes widened. "All of them?"

DJ lifted a shoulder. "I had one scare and I didn't believe it. All three of them said yes."

Harper wanted to ask what the answer had been. What had she done? Was there a little kid waiting to greet her at DJ's apartment?

Had she given it away?

Had an abortion?

Lost it?

With shaking fingers, Harper took the box that she saw on a million commercials. Early Pregnancy Test, First Response, the idiot proof test Clear Blue Easy....God, there were a half dozen on one row. Let alone the other ones for ovulation and pre-screenings. She snatched three of the main name brands off the shelf and stalked up to the counter before she chickened out.

The woman at the counter didn't say a word. Harper must have *full-fledged panic attack ahead* in her eyes or something. She didn't even hear the amount, just swiped her bank card, and took the bag out the front door. DJ ran after her.

"Hey there, psycho-girl. Wait up."

"I just want to get it over with. Please, DJ."

Her new friend sighed and simply nodded, opening her door and starting the car.

The ride to DJ's house was quiet. She could see the pink and blue boxes through the thin plastic of the bag. Easy to do, quick answers, smiling babies, and a wildly grinning woman stared back at her.

Where was the box with the terrified woman like her? The one who had rage and disappointment in her eyes because she'd been stupid? Where were the boxes with the shaking hands and women curled up in a fetal position?

Jesus. Did she have to think of fetal?

She cupped her hand over her middle and closed her eyes.

"We're here."

Harper blinked her eyes open, realizing that they'd stopped. She clambered out of the car and followed DJ up a set of cement and iron stairs. It was a typical apartment complex. Exactly like one she'd lived in with three girls while in culinary school.

DJ opened the door on the second level and held open the door. "Do you need to drink something so you can actually pee?"

Harper knotted the bag around her finger and nodded. "Yeah, maybe." She cleared her throat. "I'm sorry I'm being a freak over here. Thank you so much for helping me out."

"Don't worry about it. I've been there." DJ turned and handed her a glass. "I'm just surprised you don't have a girlfriend to call."

Harper gulped down half the glass, setting it down on the counter of the small kitchen. She had Annie, but she was vacationing with her parents. How the heck was she supposed to call with this kind of freakout? "I work with mostly men, to be honest."

"Not a hardship." DJ crossed her arms. "I recognized your husband on the first day."

Harper stopped twisting the bag around her fingers. God, she hadn't even thought about that. Since they'd gotten to Texas, no one seemed to notice Deacon under his beard.

What if she took the test and DJ called the tabloids to tell everyone? Would that be juicy information?

Deacon's band was gaining notoriety, but they were off tour and out of the public eye lately. Would anyone even care?

DJ stepped in front of her. "You need to breathe and stop worrying about shit. Just because I know your hubster is famous doesn't mean I'm going to freak out or anything."

Harper bowed her head. "We just started dealing with the fame thing. It's not like I'm with Simon. He can't even walk down the street."

"But Deacon is a big guy. People notice."

Harper's head lifted. "Exactly. Even if they don't recognize him they stare because he's so damn tall. Then the more people look, the more they think...wow—he's gotta be someone famous. And then it spirals from there, usually."

DJ leaned against her counter. "You'd think being with a famous guy would be cool."

Harper snorted. "It is, until someone literally climbs over you to get to your husband."

"I'd start swinging."

"It's easier to just get out of the way."

"I don't know how you do it. Well, I do. Because, wow, that man is fine." DJ fanned her face. "No offense, but your husband is sexy as sin."

Harper lifted her bag. "Obviously, you don't need to tell me."

DJ snickered and took the bag. She set it on the kitchen table, unpacking the boxes. "Let's figure this out, all right?"

Harper nodded and picked up a blue and white box. A few minutes later, they had all of them open and the little wands lined up. Other than the length of time it took for the results to show in the window, there wasn't much difference.

All she had to do was pee on them.

Sweet lord have mercy.

Before she could nerve up any more, she swiped all three up and followed DJ down the hallway to the bathroom.

"You good?"

She was so far from good, but she nodded anyway. She closed the door and took care of business. A few seconds later, she had them all lined up on a hand towel.

She washed her hands and dug out her phone.

WHERE ARE YOU?

She flicked away Deacon's text and set the timer for five minutes then left the room. She couldn't stare at them.

DJ poked her head around the corner. "Well?"

She held up her phone. "We'll know in a few minutes." She

popped her knuckles and paced the length of DJ's hallway. Six steps, spin, then five.

Six then five.

Her phone buzzed in her palm. She lifted it and another text bubble filled her screen.

I'M LONELY. COME PLAY WITH ME.

She curled her hand around her phone and pressed the top edge to her lips. He had no clue.

He should be here, Harper Lee.

Nerves and guilt swirled in her belly. She just needed to know then she could deal with it. She could make a game plan and sit him down to figure things out. It was better this way.

Her phone chimed and buzzed under her hand.

Time's up.

She swiped a hand down her face, lifted her chin, and pushed the door open to the bathroom.

Plus sign.

Blue line.

Positive.

Something inside her knew. As much as she wanted to deny it as stress or a late period. She'd known.

She crouched down and pressed her forehead to the front of the counter.

A baby.

Inside of her.

Deacon's baby. How was she going to tell him? Everything in their life was so in flux. They barely had their own bedroom in the house they were renting with the band. They'd barely had a moment alone, with him in the studio and her business.

They were just starting out.

Fast.

Mach speed fast. She'd fallen in love, gotten married, and started her company years ahead of schedule. How were they supposed to do this too? She had freaking whiplash, for God's sake.

"Well, shit."

Harper turned her head at DJ's voice. "Yeah. Can't get much more positive than that line up, huh?"

"I have to say, I was hoping to crack open a bottle of wine, not a ginger ale."

"You and me both." Harper sighed and stood. She gathered up the applicators. She had a feeling she would need them. Proof to stare at or to defend when she told Deacon.

Would he be happy?

His entire life was just starting. The timing on this was so beyond awful.

"All right. Let's go with plan B discussions. Are you hungry?"

Harper shook her head.

"Mind if I eat?"

She shook her head again.

DJ herded her out of the bathroom and into the living room. "Sit."

She sat because it was easier to follow directions at this point. Her brain had completely seized and a symphony of white noise had taken over her hearing. The three sticks were fanned out in her fist.

Funny how she couldn't quite put them down.

DJ sat down next to her with one of the test boxes, a bowl of grapes, and three Babybels. She unwrapped the cheese and split the wax encasing before handing her one. "Your gut has to be a mess."

"Food doesn't taste right."

"Try it."

Harper nibbled on the edge. It tasted like cheese. Thank God. She took a larger bite and collapsed against the couch.

Her newfound friend held out the box for the testing wands. "Time to come back from crazy town."

She sighed and slid the applicators into the box. "You're right."

She bit off a small piece of the cheese. "What did you do?" She nodded at the box. "When this happened to you."

"I was only a few weeks pregnant when I figured it out. I've been right where you are. Right on this couch, actually," she said with a humorless laugh. "The difference? I didn't have anyone to talk to. So, I went to Planned Parenthood. After I bawled like a baby and thought it over, I knew there was no way I could have a kid. At least not then. The guy had been king of the losers and was already long gone."

The piece of cheese Harper had managed to get down stuck in her throat.

The idea of a sterile room and nurses telling her all about her options was so...cold. Remote. Isolating.

"They've come a long way with their...technology, I guess is the best way to put it. As long as you're still in the first trimester you don't even have to have a procedure. All I had to do was take a pill."

Harper blinked and finally looked DJ in the eyes. "Like the morning after pill?"

"Kind of. Much stronger obviously, but along the same lines." DJ touched her hand. "You don't even have to tell Deacon if you don't want to."

CHAPTER EIGHT

DISTANCE

DEACON FLIPPED HIS HAIR BACK OUT OF HIS FACE. THE WATER was bracing, but it helped to clear his head. He wasn't the type to sleep into the middle of the day. Waking to find Harper gone had also thrown him off. Her note had been cryptic as hell.

Had he done something wrong?

They'd been a little off since the beginning of the trip, but he'd chalked it up to them being tired. The studio and her schedule was doing a number on their alone time, but they were making it work.

At least he thought they were.

He waded inland, relieved to see a familiar shape on the beach.

Harper's sun streaked hair was blowing around her face. She had a sweatshirt on with her little white shorts. The breeze was misty with the leftover rain showers, but not exactly sweatshirt weather. He slogged through the waves that beat against his thighs, trying to push him back into the ocean.

The flex of muscles had been just what he needed. He'd certainly been using a goodly amount of muscles with his more than active wife, but he'd missed exercising. The burn of a hard swim out in the current had wiped the last of the cobwebs from his brain.

He smiled, cupping his hand over his eyes to get a good look at her. She held up a blue beach towel, meeting him at the ankle deep waves. "There you are. I missed you."

She smiled up at him, but the crinkles at the corners of her eyes were missing.

Her polite smile.

He knew that face. Knew every curve and freckle.

He took the towel from her, swiped it over his face and chest, then his hands before tossing it over his shoulder. "What's up?"

She put her hands on his sides and tipped her face up to him. "I love you."

He cupped her face, his thumbs skimming over her slightly sunburned cheeks. "What's going on?"

Her fingers tightened on his ribs, but she didn't move closer to curl around his back like she usually did. "What? I can't say I love you, now?"

"No, of course not." He lowered his mouth to hers. The kiss was about as reciprocal as kissing a doll. He brushed her nose with his and tried again. Finally, she sighed into his mouth, her lips softening for his, her arms sliding around to his back. She rose on to her toes, opening for him. Drawing him tight to her. Suddenly, she broke the kiss and pressed her cheek to his chest, burrowing into him.

"Hey, hey. Baby," he crooned into her hair. He wrapped his arms around her shoulders, resting his chin on top of her head.

He wasn't sure what was going on, but he knew upset Harper signals. Sharing wasn't always her default reaction. Sometimes she needed to be held before she gave up the goods on whatever was bothering her. The tide rippled around their ankles and the sun was cresting into the horizon.

Content to wait her out, he simply held on. When she was like this, questions only made her clam up more. When a few minutes turned into more than ten, he started to worry.

Had he done something stupid? Had she gotten a call from Annie?

Had something happened to her parents?

Questions rolled around his head until he couldn't bite them back any longer. He pressed his cheek to her temple, brushed his lips over the crest of her cheek. "Baby, you gotta give me something. I can guarantee the stuff I'm making up in my head is worse."

She turned her face into his and he tasted the salt of her tears.

"Harper." He pulled back and cupped her face, bringing her eyes up to meet his gaze. Red rimmed blue eyes filled up with tears, starring her eyelashes. He brushed each one away as it rolled down her cheek. "What is it?"

She shook her head. "I'm just tired and I feel like crap. I don't know why I'm so out of sorts."

"Let's get you back to the cottage. There's a huge clawfoot tub that is calling your name. I'll wash your hair and we'll re-hydrate with that kickass flavored water you make with frozen raspberries. Because I am an awesome husband and went to pick up groceries while you were gone."

She gave him a watery laugh.

His chest loosened a little. That was more like it. "We can watch a crap movie and be bums."

Harper feathered her fingers through the hair on his chest. "Or, we could go home, get cleaned up, and go out to that little club you wanted to go to."

"Lawless, if you're feeling like crap, that's not going to be any fun for you."

"It'll get me out of my funk. Music always does."

"Are you sure?" He really did want to hear some music. Get out of his own head, hear someone else play. But not at the expense of Harper. She liked music, but it wasn't the heart of her like it was for him.

She hooked her arm through his. "We've been holed up here for days now. Time to go on a date, huh?"

He let her drag him up the beach to their cottage. Her smiles were still strained. Maybe they could find an intimate table, share some food, and listen to some music. It had been a long time since they'd caught a show together.

Johnny Cage's show was the last one he could think of. That night had gone remarkably well, especially when Johnny's candor about the music industry and its pitfalls had been the catalyst for so much change in his—in *their* life.

She tangled her fingers with his for a minute at the door then slipped away. "I'm going to shower off this sand."

"Want company?"

"Is it okay if I say no?"

Hurt bloomed in his chest, but he made himself smile. "Sure. Go use up the hot water. You know I like it cooler anyway."

"Thanks." She slipped into the bathroom and shut the door.

He dropped into one of the club chairs and tipped his head back. Everyone was entitled to an off day. Even on a honeymoon. But they'd had such an amazing evening. What had happened between then and now? He just wasn't sure if he was the cause or if she was just in a funk.

There was no reason for it as far as he could tell. They'd been laughing and then things had gone a bit downhill at the bar. Well, except for the whole booth thing. Christ, Harper had nearly put him in the ground with the dirty talk. She wasn't normally like that. He shifted in his seat, hardening at the memory. If he didn't know better, he was pretty sure she would have gone under the damn table. Then they'd seemed to go back to normal, a bit of much needed romance.

When the door to the bathroom opened, Deacon stood. Wide blue eyes that seemed bruised stared back at him for a moment before she broke contact and tucked her towel tighter around her. He crossed to her, coming up behind her in front of the wide mirror over the entertainment console along the side wall. Again, she wouldn't meet his gaze. Instead of saying anything more, he kissed her shoulder and went into the bathroom.

By the time he washed the sea off of him, she had dressed and pinned her hair up. This was the rare date night Harper. Gold jewelry flashed from her wrists and ears, and she had an extra layer of makeup on she only wore when they had to entertain. Tonight, she'd done something with her eyes, making them look smoky and sophisticated. Her lips were slick with clear gloss that made him want to wipe it away and leave them wet from his mouth instead.

Thin straps teased her sun-kissed shoulders, leaving her arms bare then covering the rest of her to ankles. The black and white dress looked like it was created for the beach. Loose and forgiving for skin that had seen too much skin and sand.

"You look amazing."

She smiled softly at him as she pushed one of the bangle bracelets high onto her forearm. "I'm glad I got the excuse to wear this. Jazz and I found it last month when she dragged me downtown." She turned to her cell when it chimed and Deacon swallowed his tongue. The dress was completely backless, coming to a deep U-shape at the base of her spine.

She was bound and determined to kill him today. They were social people so whether it was a meeting or a dinner to schmooze, he was used to going out with her. He wasn't used to feeling so overbearing and protective. Like he wanted to tell everyone to go to hell and keep her to himself.

He snapped out a pair of jeans from their bag and unrolled a black linen shirt. He dressed and took the extra five minutes to blow dry his hair. He didn't want to embarrass her by looking like a beach bum next to her tonight. He put down the hair dryer and smoothed his hair back. "Are you sure you want to go out tonight?"

"I've got my party dress on, don't I?"

"I can have it off you in five seconds."

"We're going out." Her voice was steady and her eyes were nearly unreadable.

Why was she trying to convince him she wanted to go out so much when it was so obvious that wasn't the case? Unwilling to push and cause a fight, he grabbed the car keys off the console. "Let's go then."

Fifteen minutes later, they navigated the small parking lot of The Muse. Murals overlapped each other on the front of the building like gang tags. Slashes of paint in bright colors over muted, dark oils mixed with spray paint making an interesting mess of pure art.

The sign over the door were letters made out of gear parts and found metals. All of it looked old and modern at the same time.

Deacon laced his fingers with Harper's and walked through the front door. No bouncer. It seemed that they were a little early. He was hoping to catch a bit of the early practice. The band was local, but very tight.

Inside, the mural motif was still going strong. The walls were much more structured. Caricatures bumped up against realistic paintings, which then manipulated dark corners with moody silhouettes depicting musicians in various moments. A trumpet player with bruised lips, but a deep and abiding love for the brass. A vocalist with a busted microphone and heart ripping out of his chest, a drummer with a kit that rivaled Neil Peart's.

"This place is awesome." He turned back to see Harper messing with the gold chain around her neck. This was completely her type of place. From the vaulted ceilings and the mismatched furniture to the old bar lining the back wall...all of it was exactly the type of place she geeked out over.

Instead, she looked almost lost. She was stunning and somehow so separate.

He drew her to him, draping his arm around her shoulders. She smiled up at him with a distracted look. She was checking out the space, and yet her eyes never lit anyplace long enough to seem to truly take it in.

Deacon led them to a small table at the edge of the dance floor. The stage was set up to oversee the dance floor. Either it would be a general admission crowd or a laid back drinks and dancing set up. He wasn't sure which one.

A waitress glided over to them, her smile bright and polite, then slid immediately into recognition. "Oh, God, you're—"

Deacon held up a finger to his lips. "My wife and I are just looking to enjoy some music tonight."

"Sure." The petite redhead in all black looked over her shoulder then back to their table. She flipped over her order booklet. "Do you think I could have your autograph?"

Deacon smiled. "Absolutely." She was totally going to tell the entire staff. Ah well. Maybe they'd leave them alone after the initial hit up for pictures and signatures. Deacon scrawled his name across the back of her pad and returned it.

She sucked on her bottom lip for a few seconds then leaned in. "Do you think you could sign it to Becky?"

Deacon's smile widened. *Look at that, a signature not going on eBay after her shift.* He took it back and wrote her name carefully and legibly, then drew a devil tail for the y.

"Oh my God, my boyfriend is going to shit."

He sat back and slid his arm along the back of Harper's chair. She instinctively turned into him, giving their waitress a polite nod. Harper was used to people interrupting them and never made a fuss. Even better, she always made the fan feel welcome. Even the rude ones that treated her with contempt.

This had to be the first time she didn't react at all.

He brushed his lips along her temple. "Do you want something to drink?"

"Nothing with tequila, that's for sure."

Deacon grinned then looked up at the girl. "Do you have flavored seltzer?"

Harper rested her hand on his thigh absently and he finally relaxed a bit. At least she was actually touching him, finally. They were out of sync, and he hated it.

Becky nodded. "Raspberry, peach, and lime."

Harper lifted her shoulder. "Raspberry."

"And I'll have whatever dark beer you have."

Becky nodded and slipped her pad into her pocket, ruffled

around in another pocket, coming out with a well used one. She scribbled down their order and disappeared.

"Are you sure everything is okay?"

"Hmm?" Harper clicked back in, leaning on his shoulder.

"I figured you'd be babbling about the decor. It's something you'd normally be taking pictures of."

She glanced around the room as if seeing it for the first time. Again she shrugged. "A bit too busy for my taste, but it's definitely rocking the multi-genre music vibe."

"It's like Jazz opened her notebook and it exploded all over the wall."

"Our manic pixie would definitely be all over this place," she said.

He bowed his head until their foreheads touched. "We'd find her in the corner, cross legged with a box of markers, drawing on the wall."

"Right." She rested her elbow on the table, tucking her chin on her hand. Again, conversation fell away.

It wasn't like he needed constant chatter. He and Harper had never been the types to fill every silence, but he'd never sat next to her and felt like she was in the next room either.

The band started unloading. Microphones, guitars, keyboard, and brass were set up in a semi-circle. When he noticed the electric violin, he sat up straight. That had been one of the additions to "The Becoming", their biggest song to date.

Maybe they needed to hit on that sound again. It brought a symphonic flavor to their music that he liked playing with. So close to the guitar and yet, so totally different.

Another layer.

He pulled his phone out and made a note and caught Harper shredding a slim, braided bracelet on her right wrist. Her rings flashed in the low light and she stopped, tucking her thumb under her ring finger to straighten her diamond. Then she curled her fingers into a fist and put it under the table.

Deacon frowned and chased her hand under the table, linking their fingers. Startled, she swung her gaze to his. The flash of something in her eyes made him lay his phone down.

It looked like...hurt.

God, had he done something? He opened his mouth to ask her again if something was wrong, but the waitress came back with their drinks and the drum tech picked then to test the skins. Harper's sudden stiff posture shut him up as well.

Instead, he gently swiped his fingertips down the smooth skin of her back, paying special attention to the dip of her spine. He kept his strokes light and soothing, but rather than calming her like it usually did, she seemed to tighten up all the more.

"I'll be right back."

Deacon sat back in his chair. "Where are you going?"

"Bathroom. Is that allowed?"

He frowned and held up his hands. "Sorry."

She shook her hair back and grabbed her purse. Her ankle length dress flowed around her as she melted into the crowd. As she practically ran away from him.

What in the holy fuck?

He lifted his beer and downed half of it in long pulls. Harper had never been the type of woman to get in shitty moods for no reason. Especially when they'd been nothing but close for the last few days and nights. Ever since she'd disappeared that afternoon, everything had gone to shit.

Letting the music distract him, he realized it had been well over fifteen minutes since she'd gone to the ladies room. He stood, using his height advantage to scan the crowd for her.

Finally he spotted her along the side wall, her face lit up by her cell phone. Who the heck was she talking to? Neither of them had even looked at their cell phones since they'd gotten to Galveston and now that was twice she'd been distracted by it. He dug his phone out of his pocket to see if she'd texted him, but nothing.

She must have felt his eyes on her, because she suddenly looked up, shoved her phone in her bag, and headed back across the room to him. Had Annie contacted her? He got the impression that Annie was going on a family vacation for the holiday since they didn't have any jobs lined up for their catering business.

When she was closer he realized he'd crossed his arms over his chest. Her shoulders were stiff and thrown back. He forced himself to relax and lifted his beer. "Everything okay? You've been gone for a while."

"Sorry. I was bored."

Deacon snapped his beer down on the table. "We didn't have to come tonight. I told you I was more than happy staying at the cottage with you."

"You know, we can do more than fuck like rabbits on our honeymoon."

He raised his brows at her biting tone. "I'm not sure if you remember who's been attacking who."

"What, are you complaining?"

His fingers curled tighter around the bottle. "No. Jesus, Lawless. What the hell? You've been stiff and defensive since you got out of the shower."

"I told you I was out of sorts."

"Yeah, I get that."

"What, is that not allowed either?"

Deacon leaned into her, his voice low. "Who were you talking to?"

"I was just checking email. Afraid I'm talking to another guy?"

Baffled, he wiped his hand down his face. "No. That didn't even occur to me. Why the hell are you trying to pick a fight?"

"I'm not."

"Coulda fooled me."

She huffed out a breath and took a sip from her glass. She turned to him and brought her hand up to his face. Smoothing her thumb along his beard, she closed her eyes and pressed her face into his neck.

Not sure what to do, Deacon slid his hand around her back. "Please, just tell me what's wrong. I know something's up."

"We've got a celebrity in the crowd tonight."

Deacon's back stiffened as a spotlight hit the table.

Crap.

"I know we're kinda putting you on the spot, but we'd love if you came up for a song. For those of you that don't know who this is, Deacon McCoy from Oblivion is here."

Deacon waved off the light. He raised his voice to be heard. "Nah, man. I'm just here to enjoy the music."

"C'mon, just one song." The guy was probably a decade older than him, but he was utterly shameless. He hopped off the stage and headed their way.

"Shit."

"Go on. You know you want to."

Deacon frowned at Harper. "We—"

"Go on. You gotta be missing your bass." She leaned into him, her eyes sad, but a little more present. "I love watching you play." She lifted her finger to the space between his eyebrows. "Quit frowning. Play me some Bad Company. You know how it twists my panties."

He almost believed her. She was smiling, but it seemed forced.

The lead singer to Burning Branch stood before him. "We can play nearly anything."

"The wife requests a little Bad Company, man."

Without missing a beat, the keyboardist started the opening strains of Bad Company's title song. Deacon shook his head and stood. Like any good bar band, the guy knew how to extend an intro.

He slapped hands to those that held them out as he walked through the tables and followed the singer to the stairs. He was pretty sure the dude's name was Rich, but he didn't want to fuck it up.

Once they got on stage, Deacon flipped his hair back. He accepted the guitar from one of the guys on stage. Instead of trying to make the strap work—he had to have custom straps made—he sat on the stool off to the side and settled the guitar into his lap.

He automatically fell into rhythm guitar, following the lead guitarist in the band. Someone from the side of the stage flew out with a mic on an adjustable stand.

The words poured out of him as natural as if he were with his own band. And when the solos became a jam and the violin came in with another richer layer, Deacon nodded in approval. It felt good to play again. Harper was right about that. Everything had become about the studio and writing and figuring shit out for the new album.

How long had it been since he'd actually just let himself play for the pure joy of it? All the things that pulled at him to create bubbled up. As if he'd simply been corked. It came out in the long drag of fingers down the fret board. On the feel of the strings under his fingertips.

These were the songs he fell back on. The ones that echoed and resonated in his chest and his gut. Pieces of him that had been drawn to the guitar and the bass from the very beginning.

One song flowed into another as "Simple Man" drifted out on the quiet crowd. He found her in the wash of faces. A magnet quick click of souls. They'd been like that from the start as well. Her name had been on the tip of his tongue for years, never knowing it was going to be Harper.

The moment he'd heard her name and felt it curl around his mouth he'd known it would be branded on his heart. They may have fought it for a while. Both of them wondering if this was supposed to work. Miles of road and infinite heartbeats later, he'd finally found what he'd never imagined to look for.

His other half.

She was exactly what he'd needed. Exactly what he'd been longing for before he'd even known what it was like to love.

Her eyes were riveted to his, but as he got a bigger picture of her in the shadows, he took in the way her shoulders slumped forward over her drink. Like she was protecting herself. He blew out a breath. His instinct was to dump the guitar and get out there. Back to her.

Why wouldn't she tell him what was wrong?

Was this what fighting with your spouse was like? He figured cranky arguments would feel different. He knew about being with people too much and how that could make you want to snarl. But everything about this felt wrong.

And when she lowered her eyes to look at her lap, breaking the contact, he felt it like a slap.

As the song wrapped up, he made his apologies when they tried to convince him to do another song. The boos were well meaning, and he gave a surprised start with the crowd clapped in thanks. Not just a polite smattering of applause, but genuine enjoyment. He couldn't even take that moment to enjoy it.

Not when he saw Harper shrink back into her chair then get up and go for the door. Rushing down the stairs, he caught Becky at the bottom of the stairs.

"I'm sorry. Is she mad at me? I had to tell my best friend and Rich heard me in the kitchen. I swear I didn't mean for anyone to know you were here."

"No." Deacon patted her shoulder. He dug into his pocket and came out with money, pressing it into her hand. "It's fine. It's not you. She's just not feeling great, and I think the crowd was too much for her."

"Are you sure?"

"Absolutely." He didn't have one fucking clue, but he knew that whatever was going on with Harper had nothing to do with the impromptu set that he'd played.

Somehow it had everything to do with him.

CHAPTER NINE

HARD TRUTHS

"Harper!"

She didn't slow. Couldn't slow down. His face, full of love, and wonder and that pure heart-on-his-sleeve passion he had for his music tore at her.

All of the things that were true and honest and important to him, and she was going to blast every single one out of orbit. They were still so new. Still finding their footing as a married couple, for God's sake.

She lifted her dress to step over the short cement divider that sectioned off the road to the access path to the beach. Cool sand sifted under her strappy sandals, spilling over her toes. She reached down and flipped off her shoes, grabbing them as she headed further down the packed sand to the water.

She needed to be away from people, from the noise and chatter of happy voices. How could everyone be so happy around her when she was so very confused?

Moonlight spilled over the sand, highlighting the tracks of seaweed and shells, stones, and the ever relentless pull of the tide as it eroded everything. Foam crisscrossed the larger rippling fingers of lapping water thanks to the stone pier and the battering ram of high tide.

She followed the moonlit path to that pier. Lonely and solitary, it made a focal point to attain.

He called her name again, gaining on her. Those damn long legs.

She couldn't ask for him to leave her alone again. She had to tell him. It wasn't right to keep the information inside her.

You don't have to tell Deacon if you don't want to.

Tears blurred her vision as she climbed the rocky pier. Sharp stones cut at her feet, her palms, her knee as she stumbled. Then his hands were there. His arms hauling her up onto the flat part of the pier where pedestrians walked.

He dragged her into his arms and the tears she'd been choking down rolled out in a torrent. She hooked her arms under his and held onto his shoulders as her nose found his chest. He smelled of ocean tinged cedar. The ever present heat of his core body temperature combating the sea spray kicking up around them, soaking her maxi dress.

He crouched down to her, pressing his nose into her shoulder, and just held her. As usual Deacon knew what she needed. Always seemed to know just what to do.

She never knew how to handle stuff. He was the problem solver. Even when he didn't know all the answers, he knew what to do.

He crushed her harder to his chest the more she sobbed.

Hormones? This wasn't the end of the world. This could be a wonderful thing, couldn't it?

Then why did it feel like such a big thing?

Why did it feel like the end of...something. Something she couldn't quite define.

She moved her arms to wrap around his neck, to press her face into the warmth that was Deacon, to find his mouth with hers. Their lips tasted of salt spray and desperation. She tasted baffled man and uncertain passion.

She tore her mouth away and rested her forehead against his. He was practically bent in half to reach down to her and the darkness put him in silhouette.

But she didn't need visuals. Earnest and bewildered Deacon would be staring down at her. But maybe it was better that the darkness cloaked them.

She wasn't sure she could take the look on his face.

Would it be wonder and excitement or would it be confused chaos?

She understood the chaos. It had been churning inside of her since that afternoon.

He cupped her face, breaking the stranglehold she had on his shoulders and arms. "Harper, you are scaring the shit out of me."

"I'm sorry," she whispered. "I'm so sorry. I know I'm not doing this right."

"Can we go back to the cottage and talk? You're shivering."

"I'm okay. I need to tell you something."

"Whatever it is, we'll deal with it."

He swiped his thumbs over her cheeks, and more tears tumbled with each pass. She took a deep breath.

Say it, Harper Lee.

Stop being such a fucking drama queen.

Say it.

Say it.

"Harper, please."

"I'm pregnant."

"What?" His hands fell away from her face and cupped her shoulders. "What did you say?"

"I'm sorry, Deacon. I swear, I don't even know how it happened."

The silhouette of his shoulders heaved once and his grip tightened on her shoulders. "A baby?" His hand dropped to the curve of her waist and across the front of her belly.

She covered his hand with hers. "I don't know what to do," she said on a whisper that barely rose above the crash of the waves behind him. "We're so not ready for this."

"This is what has you so...today. What made you so distant?"

She wrapped her fingers around his wrist, holding his hand flat to her middle. "I was lying there with you this morning and all I could think about was how crazy the last few days had been."

His fingertips widened as he splayed his entire hand along the slight indent of her belly.

"Food has tasted off for days. I just thought it was me. Strawberries were out of season. That's why they tasted like...nothing. No taste at all. Then we went and had all that greasy food. You know I love smothered fries. How many times have we gone to the diner near the new house?"

He didn't answer, and she couldn't stop her mouth from motoring on.

"The sex. I mean, God, we love sex. Obviously, we love the love part of all of this. But I've been a complete maniac. We're on our honeymoon. It's supposed to be hot sex all the time. That's not supposed to be anything different, right?"

"Except that you were so...mindless. We're usually different. Connected."

She stepped closer to him, until their joined hands were pressed between his belt and her belly. "Not the whole time. I love making love to you. Every moment of our honeymoon has been amazing."

His voice was raspy. "And you just assumed pregnant?"

"No. I had a strong feeling. I looked at my...at the app I have to keep track of my period. We're so busy, so many different things going on between the band, the house, and my job."

"So this app just says—boom, pregnant?"

"No." She stood on her tiptoes, but he didn't lean down to her.

He was stiff and unyielding in her arms.

"I went to find DJ. I needed to know. I didn't know what to do."

"You went to DJ." His voice was flat.

She rushed on. She had to make him understand. "Yes. I went straight to the bar. I didn't know what else to do. She knows this area. I hoped I could get a test. That I could confirm it."

"With DJ."

"Yes. I have them. The tests, I mean. I swear it's true." Panic overrode her need to soothe him. Maybe she shouldn't have told him.

Maybe she should have just gone to the clinic and taken care of it. Deacon didn't ever have to know. DJ was right. She should have just kept it to herself.

She didn't have to burden him with it. She could have taken care of it.

"Harper, you woke up next to me. Frightened, right?"

Dread coated her throat and mouth. She swallowed, shaking her head. Realizing it was pitch dark, she whispered, "Yes."

"I was right there. And you went to DJ."

"Deacon, I didn't want to worry you if it was false."

He stalked away from her, and the moonlight was as stark as the sun. He covered his face with his hand, dragging his fingers up and into his long hair before returning to her. Again, all in shadow. But it was too late. She'd seen the pain and shock on his face. "You thought it was something to shield me from?"

"I panicked. I didn't know what else to do."

"Why would you cut me out of this?"

His voice broke, and right then she wished for more than that flash of moonlight. Sunlight, pure and clear, would be perfect right about now. Deacon didn't break.

Until this.

She stepped forward, placing her hands on his chest. God, his heartbeat was so fast. Or was that her own pounding in her ears? "Deacon, we're not ready for this. We barely have enough strength to take care of our own issues. We're both buried."

"This isn't an issue. This is a baby."

"I know," she said.

"Our baby. You and me."

"I'm sorry." She couldn't tell if it was the baby he was upset about or her not telling him. It had only been a few hours. The news wasn't the pretty kind where you put a baby rattle on a plate, for fuck's sake.

They hadn't even discussed kids.

Kind of an important question to ask before marriage, Harper Lee. "Deacon. Talk to me."

He curled his fingers around hers against his chest. "Pregnant?"

"I know. I don't know how. I'm always so careful about my pill."

"Wow." His voice was gentle now. Shellshocked.

Harper took a shaky breath. "I never even asked you if you wanted kids."

"Do you want kids?"

"I-I..." She lost the ability to breathe. She still didn't know. "I don't know. It was never something I thought of. I'm twenty-three."

He hauled her against him, his cheek resting on top of her head. His heartbeat was the same as when he'd just come back from a run. Fast and steady.

Always steady. That was Deacon at his most basic.

But why did everything have to be so fast?

This was *so* fast.

She gripped the back of his shirt. "Deacon, you didn't answer me."

"I don't want to make you do anything you're not ready for."

"That's not an answer."

"I don't have an answer yet. You've got a couple of hours on me to digest this."

She gripped him tighter. "I understand." The tears tracked down her cheeks. She didn't know what she'd expected.

"I just wish you'd come to me first." His voice was quiet and even again yet she could still scent the pain on the air.

"I wanted to be sure."

"That's the problem, Harper. You don't have to do things alone anymore."

She drew back from him. "You knew who you were marrying. I've done everything on my own." He stroked down her hair. The familiarity of the act tightened her chest. "I'm sorry."

"I know." His voice was tired and deeper than usual. "C'mon, let's get you out of the cold."

Not willing to argue now, she let him lead her down the pier to the street. She'd lost her shoes sometime between the climbing of the pier and the beach. Once they got under the street lamp, he looked down at her and lifted her up.

"Deacon."

"C'mon, Lawless. Let me do this, all right?"

She wrapped her arm around his neck and ignored the people on the street that stared at them. It didn't matter. They didn't matter. Right now, it was about Deacon and letting him get a handle on things.

When he got to the car, he tucked her in and slid the seatbelt across her chest. For a moment, he hovered over her middle. His wide palm gently lowered to her belly before he curled his fingers in and withdrew.

She slumped back against the headrest, turning her face toward the window.

CHAPTER TEN

CONNECTION

DEACON TURNED THE IGNITION ON THE CAR AND PULLED OUT into the heavy traffic of the main strip. He didn't have any choice but to pay attention to where he was going. To focus on the street signs and the lights. To the people around him.

Anything to block out the tears he'd heard in her voice.

The panic. God, so much panic and fear.

He wrapped his fingers around the steering wheel and made himself look around. Made himself take the left, then the right that lead to their cottage.

Their destination was right there. The cozy place with the solar lights and wrought iron fixtures. The large purple door and the stone. The sweet little place that was supposed to be their escape.

He pulled to a stop at the top of the driveway and let his hands fall to his lap. Harper's forehead was tipped to the glass, her breathing regular. Had she fallen asleep?

Or was she just hiding?

Again.

He climbed out of the car and rounded the hood. When he opened her door, the dome light cast harsh shadows on her face. The bruises under her eyes and the streaks of makeup down her cheeks ripped at him.

Crouching in front of her, he smoothed a lock of hair out of her face. She instinctively moved into his touch, her eyelids twitched, but she didn't stir. As much as he wanted to shake her awake and talk, part of him was happy she was asleep.

He didn't know what to say.

Didn't know how to make this not become a fight. His hands trembled with anger and worry for her. For them.

After the word pregnant, the only thing he'd heard was *we're not ready*.

Over and over again, she'd said it. In a dozen different ways.

His worst nightmare unfolding in front of his eyes.

A woman who may never want to have his child. That was closed off even to the thought of a child in their lives. But he didn't know if she never wanted one, or if it was just because they were still so new.

And he couldn't blame her for the thoughts. That was the part that hit him hardest. Because, no, this was so far from the best timing to have a baby.

But the idea of Harper being uninvolved with the baby if they did have it?

He lowered his head.

He'd never bring a child into that kind of life.

Harper had been an independent spirit since her early teens, but at least her parents had wanted her around. She'd created a family on the road with Mitch and her brother for those times that she needed it. She'd finally let him in.

He didn't know his father. And his mother had only worried about what man would take them in, take care of her. He'd been an afterthought for as long as he could remember.

That would never be his kid's life. He or she would never wonder if he was coming home, or if he'd remember to feed them.

Deacon slid his arm under her knees and gathered Harper into his chest. His heart squeezed when she wrapped around him. Her face turned into his hair, her warm breath on his neck. The solid weight of her was real and whole.

She murmured his name in her sleep, her arms tightening on his neck.

He'd loved her for only a few months, but the idea of her not in his life was so terrifying. Why did this have to come up now? Just when they'd finally found a little peace and they were starting to actually make this marriage thing work.

He skipped the front door, not wanting to jostle her awake to get to the lock and his keys. Instead, he followed the path to the back porch. The privacy of the beach and their little cottage let them grow complacent. Locking doors was a rarity. In fact, most of the time the door was open as were the windows to let the cool ocean air in.

Slipping inside, he set her down on the bed. She rolled into the pillows with a soft sigh. He slipped off her jewelry, drew down the straps of the dress, easing the material over her ribs and down her hips. Tanned skin glowed in the low light from the bedside lamp they'd left on. She tucked her knees up against her body and wrapped herself around a pillow.

God, she was so beautiful. Her hair a tangle of sunshine streaks over honey. His eyes drifted lower to the curve of her breast and hip. Flesh colored lace hugged her ass, luring him in. He needed to hold her.

Needed to hope that they could make this work.

Intellectually, he knew she'd been scared. She'd needed proof to start to process the thought of a baby in their lives. Or...not. Ultimately, it was her body. And he'd abide by her wishes.

But the idea of losing something they'd made together sliced him down the middle. They could have children later. Women had a choice for a reason. He believed in that choice.

But could he live with it?

He turned away from her. As much as he wanted to curl around her and tell her everything would be all right, he didn't believe it.

Not yet.

Maybe not ever.

He crossed to the bathroom and shucked his clothes, stepping under the rain hood at the center of the shower. He closed his eyes and turned the water up as hot as he could stand. He reached out to the tiled wall and leaned forward, letting the water drill into his back. Until the muscles there would stop seizing up.

Behind his eyelids he couldn't help but see a little girl with blonde hair and summer sky eyes. He fisted his hands in hair and squeezed his eyes tight.

The word *pregnant* was staggering and scared him shitless.

But the next word that screamed in his head was *mine*.

My baby.

Harper's baby.

Their baby.

He slapped the controls to the shower off, stepped out, and toweled off. He returned to Harper, needing the scent of her around him. He slid in beside her, gathered her close, replacing himself with the pillow she held so tightly.

Like a vine, she slid her leg between his, plastered herself to his chest, and settled her nose into the crook of his neck. And still she didn't wake.

Right now, he wished he could lose himself in the oblivion of sleep. But he stared at the ceiling, watching the shadows slide longer as the moon traveled through the sky. Heard the seagulls cry and the crash of the tide as night faded into day.

All the while, he tried to quiet the endless record of what-ifs that spun through his head.

What if they had the baby?

Could he support them?

Did they stay in the house with the band or get their own place?

If they didn't have the baby—could he get past that?

When he couldn't stand the noise in his head any longer, he detangled himself and dragged on his running gear. He stopped at the door to the back patio and turned to watch her. White sheets and sunshine. But under the sleep was a restless frown and white knuckled grip on the sheet.

They had to talk. But first he'd take his time, as she'd taken hers. He stretched out the stiffness from staying still, holding her for hours. Forced himself to walk just long enough to warm his muscles, and then he pounded sand.

Early morning sun, spray from the shore, and the endorphin rush mixed enough that he could turn everything off. Regulating his breathing, his heart rate, his stride, all of it centered him. He ran until his lungs screamed, then he ran faster, praying for an answer or at least the hope of one. He ran until he didn't recognize the beach any longer.

Still it wasn't enough.

He turned around, aimed himself at the cottage. Aimed himself at Harper. Aimed himself to the one thing that was his peace. When he spotted the hammock and the porch, he slowed.

Then he saw her there, leaning on the sturdy post of the pergola. Her hair was down and still wet from a shower and she was wearing one of his shirts. The white Led Zeppelin one.

The familiarity of her, of the little things that made her his Harper drew him forward. He climbed the small dune to the porch and went to her. Lifting her off her feet, he closed his mouth over hers.

He felt the tears, tasted them as she gripped his shoulders, her nails digging for purchase as she shuddered through a sob.

You need to talk to her.

He pushed the voice away. He needed to connect to her again. How was he supposed to have any hope of bringing this mess to any sort of conclusion if he felt like he was moored on the other side of a sea of confusion between them?

She seemed to feel the same way because her legs came up around his hips, her ankles crossed tight to his spine. He fisted his hand in her hair, tasting every part of her mouth, branding her with everything that was inside him.

He shouldered his way inside, kicked the door shut, and kneeled on the bed with her wrapped around him. She pushed at his shorts with the heels of her feet, drawing them down as her quick fingers grasped him tight. She knew how he liked her to touch him. He groaned, wishing for even an ounce of discipline when it came to Harper. But for once, he followed his body's craving without remorse. They needed this. *He* needed this.

He dragged his teeth down her neck to her shoulder, biting the skin there until she trembled for him before he gently swiped his tongue over the same spot.

Dragging at the shirt—his shirt—he pushed and pulled until it was off and they were skin to skin. Then there were no barriers and he was there, inside of her. The heat of her welcoming body calmed pieces of him. Her hands bracketed his face and her eyes on his took him the rest of the way.

The intensity faded, and they became a slow thrust and retreat of slick flesh. She kissed him gently. Words of love and sorrow rolled between them, tripping on their tongues in between sighs of pleasure. He braced himself over her, his palm under her head to hold her close, his other hand drifting down to pull one knee up over his hip to get closer. Deeper.

Sweat coated both of them by the time he felt the first tremors of her coming for him. She curled around him until there was no room for air between them. He reared back and stared down at her as she arched up to keep the skin on skin connection.

Her eyes flew open and his name was a gasp of ragged breath. He shoved his arms under her, surrounding her as she surrounded him and buried himself deep. When her nails bit into his back, he finally let go.

When the roar in his brain stopped, he tried to move off her and she brought her legs up.

"Don't go."

"I—I don't want to crush you or..." Could he hurt her?

She cupped his face. "I want you right here. This is where you belong."

He touched his forehead to hers, moved the bulk of his weight off of her then slid down to rest his cheek against her chest. "Last night sucked."

"I know. And I'm the reason for it. I'm sorry, big guy. I handled everything wrong." She threaded her fingers through his hair with long strokes and just the tease of nails.

He couldn't help the groan. They knew everything about each other's bodies, but still hadn't caught up with the important things like communication. He dragged the back of his knuckles up her arm, catching a glint of his wedding ring. They still had their marriage training wheels on.

"*We* handled everything wrong." Unable to think about anything but crushing her or...Christ. *Baby. It's a word. Say it, asshat.* He rolled them until she was splayed across him, their legs tangled.

"I got worried when I woke up and you were gone. I'm sorry I fell asleep last night. Before we..." She laced their fingers, squeezing tight. "Before we could talk."

He brushed a kiss over her temple. "It probably worked out for the best. I wasn't sure what to say last night. I'm still not sure how to feel."

She propped her chin on his chest. "I don't either. I haven't even thought about having kids."

His chest ached at her words. "Not even a passing thought?"

Harper smoothed her thumb over his brow. "I assumed we would later. You'd make an amazing father. I already know that much." Her eyes were steady, and there was a world of truth there in her eyes. "Do you want kids?"

When her thumb curved down to his cheek and she cupped his face, he felt no shame in the blink of tears that formed. He'd always wanted a family. "You know I came from a shitty home life."

She nodded. "You don't talk about your family much. When you told me your mom wasn't coming to the wedding, I didn't want to push too hard. I should have."

He shrugged. "I wish there was something to tell. She was just... absent. We moved from guy to guy, you knew that much."

"Yeah, you told me in the truck during one of our food heart to hearts."

He swiped his free hand down her back. "I don't ever want to do that to a kid. Make him or her feel less than completely wanted." He stared up at the canopy over their four poster bed. "There were times when she forgot about me for days. Left me behind in the apartment while she partied and trolled for the next guy."

Harper angled his face back down to hers. Her eyes were white hot with a sheen of tears. "That will never be us. Ever."

"Isn't it?" He cleared his throat. "Right now, this baby isn't being celebrated." He huffed out a strangled breath. "Do you think he or she knows? Even now?"

CHAPTER ELEVEN

MR. & MRS. MCCOY

HARPER ROLLED AWAY FROM HIM. "OH, GOD." SHE GRABBED the t-shirt that had landed on the corner of the bed and crossed the room, holding onto her middle.

"Harper, wait."

She shook her head and reached blindly for the small island in the kitchen. Who could ever leave behind someone like Deacon? It explained so much. Why he was such a caretaker to all of them. Why he loved so big and so very hard.

But to think about that with *them*. With this little nebulous piece inside of her. They were so twisted up about it. There was no way she wanted him to take this on. That level of guilt.

He came up behind her, his arms folding around her gently. "I'm sorry. I'm so sorry, babe."

Would it have been better to just take care of it on her own? To have never told him? She wasn't sure she'd ever get that look out of her mind. The soul deep sadness in his eyes at the thought of her—them—not wanting this baby.

The unfairness of it rolled over her.

She couldn't do this to him.

She turned in his arms, her cheek pressed into his chest as she held on tight. She wasn't sure how long they stayed like that. Numb feet and the soft sway of them together gave her a clue that it was probably far longer than the minute it felt like.

"Part of me wishes I hadn't told you."

She heard the broken glass tone of her own voice. She stared out the window to the swaying hammock and the ocean forever rolling up the beach.

"Harper."

She could hear—*feel* the disappointment in his voice. But this was the time for honesty. "It's early into the pregnancy. There's things that can be done."

She heard him swallow, felt the race of his heart.

"You researched it already? Without talking to me?"

"No. It was DJ. She's done it." She held him tighter. "God, she made it sound so easy. And all I could think was...Deacon is just about to explode on the scene. A new album. I'm going to ruin everything."

His arms came around her tighter. "Babe." He pressed his cheek to the top of her head. "How could you think that way?"

"It's not all selfless. I'm just starting my business, too. But if there was a crappier time, then I don't know when it could be. And then... just." She curled into him tighter. "God, I'm scared," she whispered into his skin. The reassuring warmth of him right there and she couldn't hold on tight enough.

"Tell me." His voice broke and he cleared his throat. "Does the idea of a child—our child—seem so out of the realm of possibility?"

"No." She swallowed down the rocks that were currently residing in her throat. "No, Deacon. But nothing with us has ever been allowed to be planned. I met you and my entire world went into warp speed. I feel like I'm constantly running to catch up."

"I—" He cleared his throat. "Do you feel like I'm forcing you to move faster than you want to?"

"Sometimes." He stiffened in her arms. She held on when she felt him trying to retreat. "It's just because you're so sure all the time. You look at me with this complete calmness. I wish I knew how to find that as easily as you do."

He drew back so he could look down at her. "Because you are my peace. It's how it's always been. And it's something I've never had before in my life." He tipped his head down until their foreheads touched. "Maybe that's why I pushed so hard to get this ring on your finger." He pulled up her left hand and set it against his chest, covering it with his left. "I couldn't stand the thought of you not in my life forever."

"You might have pushed for a quick wedding, but I wouldn't have let you if I hadn't wanted it too." It was everything else on fast forward that made her uneasy. Sweet & Savory, her catering business, was doing well. Even with the advanced timetable, she and Annie were making something together. So much so, that she was honestly thinking about making Annie an offer to be a full partner instead of just her employee.

She was barely holding on to take care of herself and Deacon.

"What if I fuck it all up?"

"It's not just you. I'm here. I'll always be here."

If there were pictures in Wikipedia of strong, sure, capable men, Deacon would be top ten, easily. Hell, top five. But with Oblivion going on the road again within the next year, how would she be able to make it all work?

God, were the walls closing in?

She pulled away from him and rounded the island to the fridge. She pulled out the pitcher of water and opened doors. Glasses. Cups. Fucking juice glasses. Something.

Deacon came up behind her and covered her hand on the knob of the cupboard. He opened it again and pulled down two tall glasses. He gently eased the pitcher away from her and poured.

The rocks in her throat surely had to be suffocating her. Filling up her lungs. She took a deep breath, then another and swallowed more than half the glass. Rushing gulps that came out with a choke.

"I need to walk. I gotta get out of here. Outside."

Deacon pulled open the storm shutters. Clouds had come in as they were talking. The sky was steel gray and ominous. Perfect. She didn't want sun. She wanted the slap of the wind on her face. Without a word, she went for their duffel bag and unearthed her bulky fisherman's sweater and shorts.

She paused, then pulled out one of Deacon's sweatshirts. "Come with me?"

"Yes."

She nodded. There had been too many words, hurtful and too truthful between them. As usual, Deacon seemed to know that now wasn't the time to talk.

When she was dressed, he took her hand and led her out the back to the water. The roiling waves were churning with a storm to come. She didn't bother with shoes. Needing the sand and the water on her skin, if only her toes.

With linked fingers, they walked. They passed houses and hotels, one of the many piers that reached out into the ocean and groaned under the force of the gales coming in. Some of them were stone, some weather-worn wood in all different shades. Seagulls squawked and cried out as they coasted on the updrafts.

Not a soul around them.

December was off season at the best of times in Galveston, but on a day like today there was no reason to visit the beach. She was glad for it. She didn't want to exchange pleasant smiles with strangers. She didn't want Deacon to have to fend off fans today.

"We should turn back," Deacon said quietly.

She peered up at him, his hair wet ropes around his angular face. Even under the beard that tried to soften his face, there was no mistaking those cheekbones. She bumped into his solid warmth, letting him wrap an arm around her shoulders and lead her back the way they came.

By the time they reached the house, she couldn't feel her toes and Deacon, who never had a cold moment in his life, had a tinge of blue to his lips. They both stripped on the way in and headed right for the shower. She turned the glass enclosure into a ball of steam, and they both washed the sea film off of their skin. There were looks between them, but neither of them seemed inclined to touch.

When the suds from shampoo and conditioner, her body wash, and the ever perfect scent of Deacon's woodsy scent circled the drain, they both surrendered to the pull that was always between them. Deacon enveloped her with his arms and a bath sheet, bundling her close before sweeping her up and out into the living space. He dropped into one of the over-sized chairs with her in his lap. He tucked his chin on her shoulder. "We need to eat something."

Food had always been a staple in her life. She enjoyed it as much as she enjoyed sharing her recipes. Now, she gave half a damn about eating at all. She pressed her cheek against his. "So far, cheese has been the only thing that doesn't taste like all of the wrongs in the world."

"We might be in luck. When I went to the store yesterday, I got the fixings for pizza."

"Your idea of fixings, or mine?"

He huffed out a half-laugh. "Top shelf olive oil, fresh dough, and good mozzarella. Oh, and mushrooms."

"You're learning, Mr. McCoy."

"I have a good teacher, Mrs. McCoy."

The sound of that still startled her. But it was more that it sounded so right. So natural. Harper McCoy. For twenty-three years she'd been Pruitt, and she'd thought she'd be one of those women that held onto her name. But she'd wanted his name. Nothing had felt as right as writing his name after her own.

She tried to lever herself off of him, but Deacon held her there. "We're going to figure this out."

She closed her eyes and let him hug her before she stood and headed into the kitchen.

This was her domain. The cool granite top on the island cupboard steadied her like a tumbler lock being reset inside of her.

She gathered the ingredients from the fridge and found a few dried spices over the stove as well as flour in a canister. Five minutes later, she had the oven pre-heating and dough stretching on the flour-sprinkled granite top. Deacon had wandered out onto the porch as she worked, the dim light from his phone lighting his face in the growing dark.

A pizza stone was too much to hope for, but she made do with a cookie sheet. When the scents of oregano and the sauce she'd doctored didn't roil her stomach, she had hope that she'd actually be able to eat something.

She washed her hands and went for her own phone. Answered a few texts from Annie and her mom. The urge to talk to her mom hit her low and hard.

But the idea of disappointing her if she decided not to go through with the pregnancy held her back. She and her mom weren't exactly the closest of people, but her mom was as traditional as apple pie when it came to having children.

It was in direct opposition to their lifestyle, but then again...what wasn't odd in her life? She'd snuck into a costume steamer trunk at twelve just to run away with her dad. That wasn't the action of a well-adjusted child.

Adventure had been her middle name for so long. When had that changed? When she'd gotten her heart broken by Jesse at seventeen? When she'd gotten tired of climbing lighting rigs?

She set her phone down and put the pizza in the oven. When a twitter notification popped up, she flicked her phone alive again.

Come see me and Simon at the Triage Room in downtown LA
Sat night. We're guest jamming with The Purge. xoxo Jazz

Guess Jazz was getting antsy waiting at home for them to figure out studio time. She tapped her phone, staring at Jazz's name on her screen.

No.

She shouldn't burden Jazz with this kind of news.

She wouldn't be able to tell the rest of the band. It was unfair to ask her to keep a secret. Especially when secrets had done such a royal fuck-job on the band this past summer.

Harper turned off the phone and tucked it back into her bag. She put the thought out of her mind and started cleaning up the kitchen.

CHAPTER TWELVE

OPENING UP

"Babe. Come eat."

Deacon turned in his chair on the back patio. "Smells great. My gut's been rumbling since you put the sauce on." He stuffed his phone into his shorts pocket and stood.

She leaned on the doorjamb, her hair half down in one of her messy braids that she was forever bundling her hair into while she cooked. The cornsilk strands never stayed that way long. He moved to her, coasted his palm down her hair, sliding his fingers in at the nape of her neck.

"Don't look at me like that."

He bent down to her, kissing her gently. "Like what?"

"Like I'm going to break."

"You're the strongest woman I know, Lawless."

She curled her lip up in the cute little sneer that he loved and he kissed her again.

"Think you're going to be able to eat?"

"So far so good." She turned to go inside, looking back at him with an almost grin. "Evidently, tomatoes and cheese are on my good list so far."

Surprised that she actually owned up to something regarding her pregnancy, he followed her inside. So far she'd been very careful not to even discuss it as something actually happening to her. More like it was something to deal with.

It made his chest ache every time.

After spending the last half hour reading articles on the first trimester, his head was spinning with information and symptoms that now made so much more sense. Her sensitivity during sex was something a lot of women experienced. Either they were about as excited to have sex as getting waxed, or they were pretty much insatiable, with a few different levels in between.

Harper was definitely on the hypersensitive side.

Holy shit, was she ever. The first few days of their honeymoon had been a lust filled haze. Not such a bad side effect. He'd quickly sidelined into research about sex and pregnancy because...well, he'd never had sex with a pregnant woman before. They hadn't exactly been careful either.

Christ, they'd practically killed each other on a few of the rounds that first night.

But it was normal and they didn't have to worry about that until much later in the pregnancy.

If they got there.

Deacon rubbed the heel of his hand over his breast bone, pushing that thought to the back of his mind. They were still figuring things out.

He scratched his neck, his beard just on the edge of unruly. Images from all the websites and videos were playing on a loop in his head. There were videos on positions to make it good for her for fuck's sake. He didn't even want to think about the pregnancy porn out there. But beyond that, there were do's and don'ts by the truckload.

Harper got plates and put two slices on one, four on the other. When she put the two slices in front of him, he laughed.

"What?"

110

"Hungry?"

"God, yes." She folded her foot under herself as she curled into her chair. She took a bite of her slice and chewed. "Food has tasted like crap for days now. I could house this pizza by myself."

"Well, from what I've read, the food thing is pretty common. It's usually followed by morning sickness though." He lifted a shoulder. "Which you don't seem to have."

Harper's gaze lowered to her plate and she started ripping at her crust, dunking it in the extra sauce that oozed from the cheese. "What else did you read?"

He took a bite from his pizza, moaning a little before chewing and swallowing. The woman could probably make cardboard taste like heaven. "Some smells might make you nuts. Could trigger a getting sick deal."

"Great."

"Yeah. Not great, but the good part is your super nose is evidently to make sure you're not around toxins that could hurt the baby. So you kinda become the great baby protector instinctively."

Harper stood, transferring one of her pieces to his plate before returning to the kitchen.

Shit.

Fuck. Would he do anything other than bungle this stuff? He crossed the room, finding her gripping the edges of the island.

He came up behind her and caged her in, covering her white-knuckled grip. "What's wrong?"

"I've done nothing to protect this baby. What if I hurt her or him? I wasn't doing anything right for the last few weeks. No sleep..." She took a shuddering breath. "Drinking," she said on a hoarse whisper.

Deacon whirled her around into his arms, holding onto her tight. His chest constricted. They'd hit the tequila hard the other day. And they both had been enjoying her wine lessons that she'd been taking.

He'd never thought he'd be a wine drinker, but between the both of them, they were becoming quite the enthusiasts.

"Well, from what I've read...the wine deal has actually been added to a lot of doctor's okay-to-drink lists."

She sniffed. "Really?"

"Yeah." He drew her over to the bed and pushed pillows up to the headboard. He sat down, scooting back until his shoulders were resting against it. He drew his phone out of his pocket and opened his legs.

She was gnawing on her bottom lip, frowning at him.

"C'mere."

She crawled onto the bed, situating herself between his legs. They'd spent many a night on the bus like this and always ended up sliding down on either the couch or his bunk and falling asleep eventually.

He was hoping to do the same thing now.

He wrapped his arms around her, drawing her closer. Flicking his phone to life, he went to the last website he'd been reading. "This would be easier on our iPad, but I didn't bring it."

"More like Jazz confiscated it."

Deacon kissed her temple. "Because Simon busted three of them now. Idiot."

Harper scooted down, curving herself into the line of his body. "What am I looking at?"

"Evidently whatever I Google, I end up back here at this Parenthood site. And I read something about Fetal Alcohol something—"

"Syndrome."

He nodded. "But only from prolonged alcoholism. Does that sound like us?"

"I can think of someone, but it ain't us."

Deacon sighed. He had to agree with her. In their circle there was a lot of drinking, but it had never really been their thing.

He rested his chin on top of her head and started reading aloud. He felt her slowly relax. She asked a few questions, but for the most part she just listened.

Eventually her head slid down to rest along his forearm and she grew heavier in his arms as sleep took her. He read until his battery died, loathe to move and wake her.

And finally his eyes grew heavy as well and he curved around the back of her. He pressed his hand to her belly, cradling them both in his arms.

Harper woke to a furnace behind her and way too many freaking lights on. She winced as her bladder made it known that rolling over wasn't in her future.

She slipped out from under Deacon's heavy arm and reached for the lamp beside the bed and quickly extinguished the light.

"Harper?"

"It's okay. Go back to sleep."

"Where are you going?" His voice was barely a rumbling whisper, coated in sleep.

"Bathroom." She leaned down, coasting her fingers through his hair.

"'Kay." He stretched out diagonal on the bed, kicking a foot out of the sheets before rolling onto his belly like he did when he was truly out. The man could take up a bed.

She went to take care of Mother Nature's wake up call, coming back out to turn off lights as she went. The pizza was a lost cause so she left it on the counter for morning. Knowing Deacon, he'd eat it with his coffee. Her husband, the human garbage disposal.

With moonlight as her guide, she wandered around the little cottage they'd called home for the better part of a week. It held a lot of amazing memories and a lot of pain. She landed at the back door where the moon-washed pergola cut shadows against the cottage, slicing over Deacon's form on the bed.

She should crawl back into bed with him and sleep. Her brain still felt fuzzy with the few hours down she'd managed. Restlessness chased that idea away. She'd end up tossing and turning until she woke him up. A flash of light caught her eye. Her phone lit up with some sort of notification. She crossed the room, snagged it out of her bag. The lure of the hammock, waves, and fresh air was too tempting to resist.

She'd just check emails to get her mind off things. Decisions that she didn't know how to make left her brain feeling too big for her head. Between Deacon's random avalanche of trivia about pregnancy and her own knowledge of the flip side of the coin, she was on information overload.

A shit ton of email didn't help the overwhelmed feeling. So, for the first time in her life, she ignored work emails. Annie said she would take care of them while she was on her honeymoon. Instead, she clicked open stupid emails like US Weekly's barrage of celebrity gossip. She let out a soft laugh at Simon's smirky smile on the sidebar. Evidently their dear Simon had been seen out and about with some actress from a summer blockbuster movie. She actually wanted to see that movie. Uninterested in any of the other articles, she flipped back to her email.

Lost in Oblivion, Life in the Studio part 1.

She clicked on the video link and Jazz's adorable face filled the screen. She babbled about songs, about the cool studio they were working in, and was pretty much a ray of sunshine with orange strips in her hair.

Harper missed her.

Missed talking and laughing with her. It was them against a gang of guys. They had to stick together.

Before she could talk herself out of it, she flicked open her starred contacts and called Jazz. If she didn't answer, she'd just hang up.

"Oh man, you better not need bail money, Lawless."

Harper gave a soft laugh that turned terrifyingly into a sob at the sound of Jazz's voice.

"Holy crap. Harper? Are you okay? Is Big D okay?"

"I'm fine. I'm sorry, Jazz. I just needed to talk to someone and…"

"And I never sleep." Harper heard rustling, the slap of computer keys, then a muffled voice. "Okay, mama. Tell me what you need."

Harper hung her foot out and set the hammock to rocking. "I saw your video."

"Yeah? It's gotten a bunch of hits already, and the comments are blowing up." Suddenly she stopped. "Somehow I don't think you called to talk to me about my little video. Especially since you should be in prime naked time on your honeymoon. You only have two days left."

"Yeah. Things are a little bit of a clusterfuck at the moment actually."

"You guys don't really fight. What happened?"

Harper turned her face so she could see the tide and the moon-soaked beach. Should she just blurt it out? She shouldn't say anything. It sucked to get her caught in the middle of the whole thing.

"Stop overthinking and just tell me."

"I'm pregnant."

"Holy shit!"

Harper could hear her bouncing. Literally.

"Are you freaking kidding me? You guys are going to have a Mini D? Or a Mini H? Oh, man. That is so awesome. This is huge. Epic. Oh my God, I'm going to be the most amazeballs Auntie Jazz. Seriously. Do you have to be Catholic to be a godparent?"

"Jazz—"

"And wow. Seriously. You guys are going to be the most perfect parents. Can't you see D with those big hands holding on to a little baby? And hair...holy crap, between the two of you, this kid is going to be all hair."

Harper closed her eyes, unable to stop the flow of tears. That had been the one thing she kept blocking herself from doing. To actually see Deacon with a baby in his arms. For such a big man, he was nothing but graceful and gentle.

"Did you figure it out before you guys left?"

Harper sniffled. "Yesterday."

"Oh, wow. So are you like, yacking your guts out on your sex-a-thon vacation?"

"No, actually. I'm having a creepy aversion to most foods, but no upchucking, thank God." Well, except the one time at the bar, but that had been more about the horrifying realization that she'd drank so much the night before.

"So are you guys excited? Man, I'd be excited. Well, maybe not about the manster child growing inside me. Damn, girl, your guy is not tiny."

Harper slid her hand over her flat belly. Jazz was right. Deacon was not a small guy. The baby would be part her too—if she kept it.

"You're really quiet, Chef Girl."

"The timing on this isn't the best, Pix."

"What do you mean?"

She heard the honest puzzlement in Jazz's voice. As young as Jazz was, obviously with her, the thought of a baby overrode things like...*God, do I keep it?*

"You guys are going into the studio and will be touring right around the time I would have it."

"Harper, we're talking about a baby, not an *it*."

She hadn't allowed it to be a baby. It had been so much easier that way. It was a problem to solve. And now...suddenly the baby was far more real.

Deacon's voice was in her head from earlier. That the embryo was the size of a comma. That he or she would be just starting to develop. In two more weeks, the baby would be so much more.

"We—I was thinking that maybe it would be best to wait."

"You want to have an abortion?"

The word was so final. So loud and accusatory in Jazz's normally sweet voice. And then Harper bowed her head. Jazz had been a foster child. *Shit.*

Stupid, selfish idiot, Harper Lee.

"We don't know what we're doing yet. We just got married. I never thought I'd be pregnant at twenty-three."

"Right."

Jazz's voice was so soft. Harper wanted to rip her damn tongue out for hurting this girl. Even unintentionally.

She wanted to be excited like Jazz. She wanted to do cartwheels and be planning baby showers and rooms and figuring out names. And maybe she would be like that if they'd actually planned and talked about it.

But they hadn't.

And she didn't know how to feel. She couldn't match up the emotions with the huge wall of fear and dozens of what ifs.

"I don't know what to do," Harper whispered.

"What has Deak said?"

Harper felt the slide of tears down her temples as she focused on the star-strewn sky above her. Anything not to break down again. Because she really didn't know what Deacon wanted.

And she knew that was her fault.

He was taking his cues from her. And she was so completely a hot mess. Deacon only knew how to be the support guy. When had he actually ever demanded something from her?

Well, besides the caveman routine to get her to marry him. But that had been sweet and romantic in his way. And she'd loved that he'd taken charge like that. She'd never tell him that, of course. Secretly, she'd loved it. To know that he was so very certain.

It had helped make her more certain.

Maybe that's what this whole situation was missing.

Her rock was flailing just as much as she was.

"I'm going to say something and it's only because I love you guys so much. I know it's none of my business. Not really."

"I wouldn't have called if I didn't want your input, Jazz."

"Good. Because you're going to get it." Jazz took a deep breath. "This might not be planned. And I know we've talked about this over a jug of sangria a few times...but this whole crazy whirlwind you have with Deacon. It might be just your thing. Plans have their place. And sometimes the cosmos, or fate, or God, whatever you want to call it... sometimes it has other plans."

Harper set the hammock to swaying again. "Maybe it does. I never thought this crazy life would give me Deacon."

"Maybe fate is giving you a family now because it's time. Not the one you planned, but the one that is perfect for you in the end." When Harper didn't immediately respond, Jazz cleared her throat. "Just a thought."

"I think I needed to hear that. Thanks, Jazz."

"Whatever you decide to do, you've got me in your corner."

"You're pretty amazing, you know that?"

"You got that right, mama."

"Oh, and Jazz?"

"Yeah?"

"I hate to ask—"

"You don't even need to. Your secret's safe with me until you're ready to tell the masses."

"Did I mention you're amazing?"

"You may have." She laughed, and the pure light of Jazz happy filtered through the phone.

Harper said her goodbyes and pressed her phone to her chest. She watched the stars for a while, rocking herself into a calm that she hadn't felt in days. As the sky lightened and the stars lost their pinpoint luster, she finally stood and returned inside.

She slid into bed, immediately comforted by Deacon's warm body. Instinctively, he curled around her, and their joined hands covered her stomach.

CHAPTER THIRTEEN

HONEYMOON 2.0

DEACON CLEANED UP THE LAST OF THE PIZZA FROM THE NIGHT before. Pouring the second mug of coffee had him feeling a little bit clearer. Harper hadn't moved from the middle of their bed. She'd made a strange little cocoon in a patch of sun, practically pushing him out of bed.

He didn't have the heart to wake her. Not when she hadn't really slept the last few days. He was itchy to run out the last of the cobwebs in his head, but didn't want her to wake alone.

So, he would wait.

And try not to be creepy guy watching his wife sleep.

At least try. He had yet to look away from her for more than five minutes. He was seriously going to need an hour with his heavy bag and weights when he got home or he was going to go out of his mind.

"Is that coffee?"

Deacon paused with his mug at his lips. "Maybe."

"That very fine ass of yours should bring me over a cup."

He went to the coffee maker and pulled down a teacup, fixing it the way she liked. He'd read that pregnant women should limit their caffeine intake, but he didn't want to start the day off with them in the shutdown mode of the other day.

So...compromise. Small cup.

"You know, it shouldn't be cute when you objectify me like that. And yet." He crossed the room.

She peeked over the down comforter she'd confiscated sometime through the night. "Well, I wouldn't drool so much if you didn't work out like it was your job."

"Want me to stop? Get fat and sloppy?"

"Knowing the fairness in this world, you'd probably just get skinny."

He grinned down at her and held out her coffee. That was exactly what would happen. He'd been a skinny fuck until he discovered the gym at seventeen. But she didn't need to know that.

Harper's hand came out, snatching the cup, her blue eyes meeting his. "What if I do?"

He lowered himself to the side of the bed before his feet went out from under him. "Are we speaking hypotheticals here?" he asked carefully.

Harper looked down at her cup. "Deacon, what if I wanted this baby? Would you be on board with that?"

Yes.

Holy fuck, yes.

He couldn't hear around the litany in his head. Hadn't known that he'd wanted her to say those words so very badly.

"I would move heaven and earth to keep you happy."

Harper rolled onto her knees and put her cup on the bedside table. She inched over until she was in front of him, her hands on his chest, her eyes direct and intense. "That's not what I asked."

"Yes." His chest heaved. "Yes, I want this baby." He leaned into her until their foreheads touched. "I never want to put pressure on you to do something you don't want, but God, yes."

From the moment she'd said *pregnant* he'd felt sucker punched. In the dark of that pier, with a storm coming up on them, he'd lost his breath and hadn't quite ever gotten it back. The idea of a family had been a nebulous one. In the hazy future. Every day since she'd told him, it got clearer.

Amazingly, Harper's arms came up and around his neck. She caught his mouth in a desperate kiss. Again he tasted tears. He pulled her back. "Hey, hey, hey." He cupped her face. Tears starred her lashes and dripped down her cheeks. But there was a smile there.

A huge smile that had been missing for days.

"How the hell are we going to do this?"

He brushed his nose against hers. "Together. Just like we do everything else." Someday she'd believe that without him having to convince her. "We'll figure out a game plan. You're not alone anymore. You'll never be alone again."

"All I could think about was how hard it was going to be. I didn't even let myself think about a baby. And last night, all I could think about was the baby part. Of course a crazy conversation with Jazz helped too."

He brushed her hair away from her face. "You called Pix?"

She nodded. "God, you should have heard how excited she was. She scared the crap out of me talking about how big you were and how big the baby might be."

Deacon's eyebrows snapped down. "Jesus." Harper was tiny as hell. "I—"

"Any clue how big you were when you were born? Ballpark figure."

Deacon scratched his head. "Uh...I think I was nine pounds maybe?"

"Of course you were."

"But we might have a girl." In his head all he could see was a girl. "Your hair and smile, my dimples. She'd rule the world."

She laughed, swiping away tears that were still free-flowing down her cheeks.

"Are you sure?" He hadn't meant to blurt out the question, but they'd run the gamut of emotions for the last few days. He didn't want regret. Not when the happy high faded and things got hard. Because it was going to be hard.

"I'm sure about you. I'm sure about us. I'm sure I'm going to be a maniac," she said with a hiccupping laugh. "I love you, Deacon. Everything about us has been in fast forward and it's scary as hell, but maybe that's what makes us work." She tucked a wavy lock of his hair behind his ear. "If the world let me overthink everything, look at what I'd miss."

He hauled her into his arms, kissing her until the tears were sealed in with happy laughter. He rolled them back onto the bed that smelled like peaches and cocoa butter. Into the bright sunlight that lit up the white so it was almost blinding. He rolled under her, dragging her up to straddle his chest, her knees jammed under his arms. He lifted her shirt to see the tanned expanse of her flat stomach. She held the shirt up as his fingertips feathered over her sides, while his thumbs stroked the downy smooth skin on either side of her belly button.

So many changes were coming. He'd freely handed this woman his heart. He thought that had been an incredible feat. And now he'd found out he had so much more waiting in reserves. There was an incredible love growing inside him for someone who hadn't even arrived yet.

Harper covered his hand, dragged his palm up to her breast to cup it. The heat from her nipple instantly pushed any thoughts of babies to the back of his mind. He swiped his thumb over the tight tip, then tugged just the way she liked.

And as he'd discovered, her hyperactive sensitivity brought things to another level. Only this time he knew what to expect and just how to take care of her. She sighed, her head tipped back as he continued the soft caress. He pushed her shirt higher, burrowed under to replace his hand with his mouth. Hot silk skin came alive under his touch. He circled her nipple, but avoided the tight center. He moved from one to the other, taking his time to taste her everywhere except that exquisite tip. She growled out his name as she gripped the headboard with her free hand. "You're killing me."

He finally sucked her deep into his mouth, taking as much as he could. He pushed up her shirt from the back until she helped him and flipped it over her head. She inched down his chest, but he wouldn't let her pull away just yet. The little sounds in her throat were driving him crazy.

He caught her gaze as he let her nipple pop from his mouth. The blue of her eyes were a mere sliver. Her pupils were wide open, drowning in lust. A siren's call couldn't have lured him more. But he didn't want that today. He wanted the playful Harper full of laughter.

He slowed his kisses, cupped her breasts gently as he blew lightly on the tight tips. She closed her eyes, his name a long, slow groan. She rested her forearms next to his head until her breasts pressed into his chest. She sighed as he cupped her hips, his hands sliding lower to her ass.

"I'll tell you one thing." She wiggled lower until she straddled his straining cock. "This increased libido thing. Awesome," she said with a purr.

He ground his molars together. "You're killing me."

"I think you can handle it."

Oh, he'd handle it. Morning, noon, and night if he needed to. When she pushed at her panties, fumbling to get out of them, he lifted his hips to get rid of his shorts. Without warning, she guided him inside her. He slammed his head back against the pillows, watching as she took all of him in one sure stroke. She levered herself up, her hips undulating as she rode him slowly.

He bracketed her hips, but let her set the pace. Sunshine sex was officially his new favorite kind of sex. His grip tightened as her tempo increased. She arched her back, tipping her head back in abandon. He glided one hand up to cup her breast, plucking at the tip until he heard the revved growl that told him she was close. He could have easily let her go right then. She was so damn close that it would only have taken a light stroke against her clit and she'd have shattered above him.

But he didn't want it to end quite yet. He rolled them both, never missing a thrust. He wanted her mouth, wanted her taste inside of him and around him in the blast of sunshine with her laughter. He rolled his hips, laughing when her eyes went wide and she hooked an arm around his neck. She dragged him down as he went deeper then shallow.

"You freaking tease," she said on a shaky breath.

"You got it. I missed you, Harper. I don't want this to end yet."

"Are you kidding? We've got two more days of this." Her voice broke as he slipped his fingers in between them.

"Two more days," he panted. "We'll kill each other."

"Honeymoon reboot. I'm all for it."

"Christ, yes." He hooked her knee over his hip and drove down into her. "God, you feel too good."

Her nails bit into his back. "If you stop again, I'll never made those strawberries again."

"Now that's just mean." He smiled down at her and circled her clit with his thumb until she shook, until she screamed, until his name was a hoarse cry. When he couldn't hold back any longer, he rode out her last orgasm and let go. When her legs slid limply to the bed and he managed to catch his breath, he couldn't hold back a wheezing laugh.

"I should ask why you're laughing, but my thigh is still shaking from that last whopper of an orgasm. So, I gotta say, I just don't care."

He dropped to the bed beside her, his fingers sliding over her, unable to stay away from her.

She moaned and tried to curl into herself. "Ever heard of the term *open nerve*?"

He gentled his touch. She was slick with him and her combined. He lowered his mouth to her breast, sucking lightly as he teased her to the brink again. Her release was long and sweet. The kind that had started on a bus with two people fumbling into love. And now the

124

love had created something new and exciting. He took a mental snap-shot of the day. Sunshine and Harper. Love and forever. Wife and the future mother of his child.

He didn't know exactly how they'd get to the end of this new road, but it was the start of something amazing—that much he knew.

CHAPTER FOURTEEN

CH-CH-CHANGES

"I MISS THE BEACH ALREADY." HARPER RUBBED HER HANDS together as they walked up the stairs to the house in the Hollywood Hills. More Christmas lights had been added to the railings since they'd been gone, as well as a fat wreath with a huge purple bow. It was also at least twenty degrees colder than Galveston. The last two days of their honeymoon had been unseasonably warm and perfect. So perfect she'd contemplated staying right there through the New Year.

Damn responsible nature had killed that idea.

Deacon opened the front door, dumping their duffel bag into the mudroom. The thing was filled to the brim with sand no matter how many times she'd shaken out their clothes. Music blared from the living room then went silent.

Harper grinned up at Deacon when she heard Jazz's loud whisper for everyone to be quiet. She took his hand, dragging him into the living room.

"Surprise!" Jazz held up a sign that said, "Welcome home" with precisely seven exclamation points after it. One for every color of the rainbow.

Nick had a party horn sticking out of the side of his mouth. His face was deadpan as he blew into it, making the stupid party favor shriek. "Congratulations on fucking for a week straight."

"God, you're such an ass." Simon rose off the couch, two party hats on his head like horns. "It's congratulations on *making love* for a week straight." He waggled his eyebrows. "As dirty as possible." He crossed the room and shook Deacon's hand, then pressed a smacking kiss on Harper's cheek. "Way to go, blondie. You look sassy and happy."

Harper rolled her eyes. "Gee thanks, Simon." But she was happy. Still freaking out every other hour or so, but definitely happy.

Gray gave them a halfhearted salute from the couch. "Welcome home, guys."

Jazz bounded over to them, hugging them both before taking Harper's hands and dragging her to the couch. "Tell me everything."

Nick reached next to the sofa and pulled out his acoustic, settling it into his lap. "Are we going to get a blow by blow about the whole week? Because if we are I'm going upstairs. I'd rather watch Guitar Center."

"Then go, Mr. Rude," Jazz said.

Nick huffed, but kept his mouth shut and strummed his guitar. Harper didn't recognize the song. Maybe they'd actually gotten some writing done while she and Deacon had been away.

Deacon popped his knuckles. "Actually, this is really well-timed. I didn't think I'd get all of you together at once before tomorrow. And I don't really want to talk about this in the studio."

Jazz tucked her feet under her legs and couldn't stop bouncing.

Simon quirked an eyebrow. "Care to share what's turning you into the human vibrator?"

Jazz stuck out her tongue. "Not my news to tell."

Nick stopped strumming. "Should I put my guitar down for this?" He pulled the cigarette out from behind his ear and stuck it in his mouth before taking it out again to flip it around at the filter.

Harper moved next to Deacon, linking their fingers. "We're doing this now?" she asked him out of the side of her mouth.

Simon climbed onto the couch and perched on the back support. "This better be good. I have a very dirty woman waiting for me who's been sexting me for the last hour."

They'd gone over how to tell the band at least fifteen times since they'd woken up that morning. She opened her mouth to ease them into it like they discussed.

"We're having a baby," Deacon blurted.

Or they could just spit it out. "That is not how we rehearsed."

Deacon's cheeks flushed. "Sorry."

Jazz popped off the couch and jumped into Deacon's arms. She wrapped her legs around his waist and levered herself up to kiss his cheek. "This is so great." She jumped back down and tacklehugged Harper. "So, so awesome."

Nick looked from Deacon to Harper, then swung his gaze to Jazz. "Are you high? We're a band. What the hell you so amped about the idea of a baby on a bus for?"

"Hey, watch it." Harper's voice rose.

Nick turned on her. "What, it's not enough that you guys are married? You gotta bring a kid into this? Now?"

All strong and valid points that she'd lived with for days now. Except everything was different now.

Deacon stepped in front of her. "Look, man, I know it's not ideal."

"Ideal? Holy shit, D. What the fuck?"

Harper pushed past Deacon and stalked to Nick. "This wasn't planned, but you know what? We're dealing with it. We're having it. There is no discussion here. I realize this will make things difficult scheduling wise—"

"Difficult?" Nick paced the room. "Difficult is adding a sixth person to the bus. Catastrophic is a fucking...what do you call it? A goddamn playpen."

She felt Deacon seething at her back, but she held up a hand to him. "You don't think we've thought of that? That *I've* thought of that? The baby wasn't planned, but it's a reality. Our reality."

Nick collapsed back onto the couch. "What the hell happened to my band, man?"

Jazz plopped down next to Nick. "It became our band. Now more than ever."

Simon crossed his arms and walked over to Harper. "So, a baby?"

"A baby," she confirmed.

He nodded. "Can I borrow it sometimes? Chicks really dig babies. Makes them think I'm all sensitive and shit."

Harper laughed. "No way in hell."

Simon gave her a pouty face. "I'll wear you down."

Deacon looked at Gray. "What do you think, Vapor?"

Gray crossed his arms over his chest. "It's going to be an interesting tour."

Deacon gently gripped Harper's shoulders. "Never liked boring anyway."

Gray gave a rare smile. "But I'm happy for you guys. This is good news."

Jazz hopped off the couch and went to the side drawer. She waved a book at them. "I've been doing some reading."

Nick flipped open his Zippo and slammed out the back door, a puff of smoke in his wake.

Harper gripped Deacon's hand on her shoulder, leaning into him. "Not quite as bad as I thought."

Deacon wrapped an arm around her waist. "Impressive mama bear growl there at Nick," he said low into her ear. "That was hella hot."

She laughed. "You're a sick man."

"What? I like when you get all territorial about our kid. It's pretty awesome."

"Nick brings it out in me."

Deacon snorted. "He brings it out in most people."

"So it says here that your boobs get sensitive. Like, you can have an orgasm just from sucking on the nipples sensitive." Simon looked up from the baby book Jazz had apparently handed him. "Is that true?"

"That's the first question you ask me?"

Simon shrugged. "Sounds like a perk to me."

Gray gave a soft snuff of a laugh before standing up. "I'll be back later."

Jazz looked up from the book, elbowing Simon out of the way. "Where are you going?"

"Out." Gray grabbed his coat from the closet. "Don't wait up."

"What was that about?" Deacon asked as the door closed.

Jazz brought the book to her chest, arms wrapping tight. "He never stays home anymore."

Harper frowned. Definite undercurrents there. "You okay?"

"Sure." Jazz sighed, opening the book. "I am now."

Harper linked her arm through Jazz's and peeked over her shoulder. "So, tell me what you've learned." She listened with half an ear as she watched Deacon go out the back door. She hoped he could talk Nick down. A lot of changes were going to happen. She didn't want to cause another rift within the band. This baby was happy news no matter how Nick reacted. Jazz's cheerful chatter helped support that.

A few minutes later, Deacon returned with a tiny shake of his head.

Nope, Nick wasn't ready to talk evidently.

Deacon sat next to her, both he and Jazz spouting off information about babies and pregnancy like they were in a trivia contest.

When Simon sat on the other side of Jazz, a purring George in his lap, Harper finally relaxed a little. This family she'd married into wasn't exactly what she'd envisioned for herself. But like the baby that was now a part of her, so were they. And she wouldn't change a thing.

*Turn the page for a sneak peek at **TWISTED** book 2 in our LOST IN OBLIVION series, available now!*

TWISTED

Chapter 1
Then

"Gray, your new sister is here."

Gray rolled over on his stomach and dragged the pillow over his head. He was still hungover from the party last night and wasn't in the mood to play nice. Not while there were cymbals crashing in his skull. "Can I talk to her later?"

"No. You can talk to her now."

He groaned. "Brent's home for the weekend. Let him play welcome wagon. I'll take the night shift."

"Brent already went back to campus."

Figured. His older brother swung in for a night then swung back out again before the fawning stopped. Leaving everything to Gray as usual.

"Besides, I think you're more suited in this case." The mattress sank as his mom sat down at his side. "This one's not had an easy time of it. I think a friend would do her good."

Instantly guilt twisted in Gray's already knotted stomach. Damn Mad Dog. He was never drinking that crap again, no matter how often Jimmy tried to tell him getting loaded would help their band. Bullshit. All it had done was given him a fucking headache and put him in a pisser of a mood. He rolled over and tossed his arm over his eyes. "How bad?" he asked tiredly.

"Pretty bad. Her mom kept her sister but turned Jasmine over to the state. Said she'd gone wild and she couldn't handle her anymore. Since then, she's bounced from place to place."

"So she's trouble." He didn't have time for that. He could stir up enough of his own.

"I think she's just lonely. You have to meet her."

The foster kids his mom and dad took in had usually come from rough environments. Some of the children were friendlier than others, which was understandable. It had been six months since the last one, and he'd begun to think that the Duffys had taken in their last kid. Brent was off at college now, and he would be too in a couple of years. Maybe his parents were looking forward to their empty nest.

But now they'd taken in Jasmine.

"Jasmine, huh? Like the flower?"

"Yes. Jasmine Edwards. You two actually have a lot in common."

He snorted. "Oh yeah? Like what?"

"You'll see." She stood up. "I'm going to give you two some time alone. I'll be in the den, okay?"

He grunted and waited until she left to haul his ass out of bed. He checked his appearance in the half bath off his bedroom. Lovely. Bloodshot eyes, check. Way too long hair that looked like someone had gone at it with shears, check. Dragon breath from puking in the bushes before he'd crashed that morning, triple check.

He brushed his teeth a couple of times, pushed a hand through his hair and sniffed his Dokken T-shirt before taking another run at his pits with his deodorant. Good enough. He headed downstairs, taking the steps two at a time. It wasn't like he was meeting anyone he needed to impress.

Five minutes with this chick and he could consider his duty done. Then maybe he could get some practice in on Krystal Sword's new material. He'd been writing this new song—

Halfway into the living room, he came to a halt.

Everything stopped. His feet, his breath, his heart.

Curled up in one corner of the couch sat a tiny brunette, a guitar stretched across her lap. It dwarfed her, making her seem even smaller. Her fingers moved like a blur, coaxing out the most beautiful music from the antiquated acoustic. Scratches and welts covered the cherry wood, but it didn't matter. She might as well have been playing the finest instrument that ever existed.

Head bent, she strummed and sang a song about a woman on her wedding day. Hope, fear, excitement. Crying tears of joy. He didn't know the song—folksy type music wasn't his thing—but he couldn't stop listening. Or watching the way her perfect pink lips curved around the words she sang so effortlessly that she became one with the melody.

When she finished, she glanced up and flushed. "Oh."

Her eyes were bright blue, like the sky on a sunny day. Surrounded by blue-flecked lashes, those stunning irises bored into his and left him mute. He couldn't say a damn thing.

"I'm sorry. I guess I shouldn't have been playing." She set the guitar aside and brushed her hands over her skintight white jeans. The denim had been sliced all the way up and down her legs, and through the holes he could see glimpses of color on her skin.

He cleared his throat. "Tattoos?"

Her flush only worsened as she followed his gaze to her legs. "No. Markers." She pulled open one of the gaps on her knee and a drawn-on daisy appeared in the hole. "When I get bored, I draw on my clothes. And on myself, since I'm easier to wash off." She gave a little hitching giggle and stood up, sticking out her hand. "I'm Jazz. You must be Gray."

He clasped her hand, not the least bit surprised when heat flared between their palms. But she didn't seem to notice. She just kept smiling at him, her huge eyes locked on his.

"Yeah." He swallowed hard. "I'm Gray."

"Nice to meet you. How old are you?"

"Sixteen." Not for too much longer though. "You?"

"Fourteen. But I feel way older."

He looked her up and down. "You don't look older."

She threw back her shoulders. "Yeah, 'cause I'm little. But I could still grow. It could totally happen. I take my vitamins. I work out." She flexed her tiny biceps under the pink sleeve of her T-shirt and he couldn't help grinning.

"Sure. I bet you'll end up six-feet tall."

"Nah. That's as tall as you are. I'd settle for five-two."

Gray glanced down at her red Chucks. "You could wear heels."

"No way." She scrunched up her perky nose. "I'd rather be short."

He laughed and gestured to her guitar. "So how long have you played?"

"All my life."

He tried to take a deep breath and realized his lungs were still seized up like he'd just run a mile. God, she was cute and she was into music? And she'd be living in his *house*? *Down, boy.*

Talking to chicks wasn't difficult. Well, before today. He'd never had any trouble acting cool around them in the past. Besides, this one was too young. Fourteen-year-old girls weren't going to be as easy to coax up into his bedroom, something he did on the regular. He loved girls. The way they smelled. Tasted. Felt under his hands. They were like guitars, all smooth lines and perfect curves. He adored pulling different sounds out of them, just like he did his axe.

But this particular one would be his sister. Sort of. Which made this awkward.

"Me too. I'm in a band," he said, preening a little.

"You play too?" Her eyes lit. "What instrument?"

The nerves finally disappeared as he slid his hand down the neck of her guitar. The wood felt good under his hands. Like it was meant to fit his grip. He grinned. "Guitar."

NOW AVAILABLE!

For more details please visit www.rockerreads.com.

LOST IN OBLIVION SERIES

Have you read all the books in our Lost in Oblivion Series? Each book can be read as a standalone, but to enjoy the series the way we intended, this is the reading order.

GIFTED (*book #4.2*)
MERRY OBLIVION (*book #5.2*)

ALSO BY CARI & TARYN

FOUND IN OBLIVION

a Rockstar Series

Bedded Bliss #1

Triple Trouble #2

Dirty Duet #3

Lost Lyric #4

Perfect Pitch #5

Raw Rhythm #6

Coming Soon

Finding Forever #7

HAMMERED

a Rockstar Romantic Comedy Series

Manaconda #1

Manhandled #2

Manipulated #3

Maneuvered #4

IF YOU'D LIKE MORE INFORMATION ABOUT THE SERIES & EXTRAS,
PLEASE VISIT WWW.ROCKERREADS.COM.

ABOUT THE AUTHORS

USA TODAY BESTSELLING AUTHOR *CARI QUINN* likes music and men, so she figured why not write about both? When she's not writing, she's screaming at men's college basketball games on TV, playing her music too loud or causing trouble. Sometimes simultaneously.

USA TODAY BESTSELLING AUTHOR *TARYN ELLIOTT* is obsessed with rock stars, men, and her unending playlists—maximizing these things seemed like a very good idea. When she's not writing, she's losing hours to hot men on TV, and/or a graphic design project. Multitasking is her middle name.

They decided to combine forces and found that hey...this writing deal is even more awesome when you collaborate with your best friend.

AND SO **THE OBLIVION WORLD** WAS BORN.

Want to know more?
rockerreads.com
taryncari@gmail.com